FIELDS OF LIES

A SEACROSS MYSTERY

SABINA GABRIELLI CARRARA

THE GREEN BAT

ISBN-13: 9781916266001

Cover by Cover by Debbie Boettcher www.indiebookcovers.weebly.com

Aknowledgements

Thank you to my daughters for their support and enthusiasm, and to my husband who silently but patiently stayed by my side during this journey.

To my friend Sara Jane, who pushed me out of my shell and never stopped believing in me.

CONTENTS

1

Bernadette was lying in bed awake, waiting for the alarm to ring. There was a time when she'd dread the ringing of the alarm clock but after the finding, it was a relief. The click before the ringtone was her signal to get up and start keeping herself busy, to not think about what happened, and continue pretending everything was alright and that she was not living in fear of the police knocking at her door. It all started innocently. She thought she had everything under control and that the present was far stronger than the past. But soon, there were memories and feelings — feelings she thought she had buried forever, twenty-three years ago. Except she hadn't. She had been weak, and now; everything was at stake, as her secret was no longer safe. She had been naive to think she could make amends with the past without endangering the future.

That morning, Michael left earlier than usual, and Bernadette didn't even wonder why until he left. He had probably told her, and she was most likely not listening, there were too many voices in her head lately. She'd got up with him and made him breakfast as usual. Breakfast used to be their precious time together before the madness of work and school runs started. Even though the days of school runs were long gone, Bernadette continued to get up with Michael every morning to make him breakfast. Nothing fancy, just some fresh brewed coffee and a few pieces of toasts with peanut butter — not the most popular choice for breakfast, but they both loved it. It was the first thing they discovered they had in common and she used to joke that they fell in love over a jar of peanut butter. Over the years, having breakfast together had become more of a habit filled with mutual comfortable silence than a special time filled with chats stolen from the frenzy of life. The toaster spat out the four slices of bread; and she brought them to the table where her husband was waiting with his knife already dipped in the blue jar. They had their coffee and toast and when he was done, Michael patted the dogs on the head, kissed his wife on the forehead, and left. That kiss on her forehead — that once would have gone unnoticed, as much as the silent breakfasts — was now something to think about. There was a time when her husband hugged her and kissed her passionately before leaving, never mind if it was for the day, a week or just a few hours. There was a time when there was no silence between them. What happened? And most importantly, when did it start? Was it her fault because she stopped pretending? Was he finally tired of living a lie? Or, maybe it was just a kiss on her forehead, and she was just imagining things — a guilty conscience could easily do that. Maybe she was changing and not them, not him. She couldn't say Michael was distant or neglecting her, that would have been untrue, but he was not her lover anymore. It was too long since his strong hands had pulled her toward him vigorously and kissed her like it was the last time.

"So, now you are saying it's his fault?" the voice inside her head cried out. She was in a way, but was it the truth or was she simply justifying what she had done? Bernadette knew the answer very well but refused to admit it. The loyal and understanding Bernadette was now on the wrong side. The last few weeks had changed her. She had not decided if it was for the better, but could not stop wondering if things would have been different had she not seen what she had. Were the possible consequences of her role in what she had witnessed the only reason she was now contemplating what to do with her life? Of only one thing she was certain, she couldn't undo what was done or change her feelings. Bernadette brought her tea in the garden and sat on the bench beside the big yellow rose, the one she had replanted from her parents' garden after they sold the house. For some reason, it made her feel safe. Over the years, it became her favourite spot in the garden; a place where she could go when she wanted some peace, even though "peace" had recently become an empty word. In the last weeks, Bernadette was restless and certainly had a lot to think about, but did not have much peace. The morning was sunny and bright, but the air was crisp. It was nearly mid-October, and like her mum's rose, even the hydrangeas were still in full bloom. Autumn has always been her favourite season. She liked the shorter days, the light of dusk, and the festive Halloween atmosphere. Michael always mocked her for being more excited about Halloween than their son had been. Her head was now filled with old images and memories of Samuel as a child going trick-or-treating with her, both proud of their costumes. Thinking about Samuel made her feel even more guilty and alert because, like his father, he probably would never forgive her. A shiver ran through her whole body, absorbed in her thoughts. Bernadette didn't realise how much the temperature had dropped. She tightened her cardigan around her waist and went back inside.

2

(THE DAY OF THE FINDING)

Her hands were shaking, and she dropped her keys twice before she could slide them into the padlock of the pedestrian's gate.

"Hi, Bernadette! A lovely day for a walk, isn't it?"

Walking with her head down and desperate to reach the safety of her home, Bernadette had not noticed Mrs Hazel, the elderly lady living in the cottage up the road from her. She liked her neighbour, and always stopped for a brief chat with her. She was cheerful, kindly, old-fashioned and generous enough to share the secret of growing magnificent bushes of roses like those now covering most of her front wall. Mrs Hazel was getting closer and Bernadette could see her shadow right behind her. With the full intention to discourage any interaction, she raised her arm to wave and didn't turn. Bernadette was not used to being rude to anyone, let alone to a lovely old lady, but today she couldn't stop and talk to anybody—not while she was wearing a blood-stained blouse. The red stains on the white silk would be impossible to miss. Once inside the house, Bernadette realised she also had blood on her hands and went straight to the kitchen sink to wash them. Then, she went back into the hall to check her keys for traces of blood, as well as everything she had touched. The keys looked fine, but the keyring was visibly stained; so was the handle of the main door. She wiped the blood from the door and tried to clean the keyring, but because it was leather, it had absorbed the blood permanently. With rushed and compulsive movements, Bernadette removed the keys from the ring and went to throw it into the black bin outside. Hopefully, her friend Jane wouldn't notice she was no longer using the bear-shaped keyring she had given her last year for Christmas. Her dogs, Pedro and Berta kept following her impatiently. She had no time for them either, and so she fed them their dinner just to keep them out of her way. She glanced at her watch; she didn't have much time to clean herself up before Michael's return. She ran upstairs, undressed and stepped into the shower. She scrubbed her body repeatedly until her skin was red and sore, but there was much more than the blood to wash away.

3

Since Bernadette and Michael's move to Seacross, neither of them regretted their city life.—This was where Bernadette was born and bred. It was the town she was somehow forced to leave so many years ago. On the other hand, Michael was a Dubliner and had lived in a central area of the city all his life, except for his summer holidays which he spent in Seacross with his family. It was during one of those summers he first met the girl who would eventually become his wife. They had met twenty-four years ago on the North Strand beach. Bernadette was with Shane Flynn at the time. She barely noticed the tall city guy with his blue eyes that he couldn't keep away from her. She and Shane had a future together, and in her heart, there was no space for anybody else. The summer ended and Michael returned to the city, with the girl with wild red curls residing in his mind and troubled heart. For him, it had been love at first sight; for her, he didn't even exist. However, a game of destiny that winter made their paths cross again, and that girl with the wild red curls was free, finally. Free to be his. Soon, Michael realised that little was left of the light-hearted creature he had met the previous summer, who had danced at the moon on the beach. Her *joie de vivre* no longer left her eyes sparkling. She was broken, but he didn't care; he took her in and fixed her. He wanted her despite everything. He made her secret his, and when they married, he felt he had finally won her over. He thought she was ultimately his, and she always acted as if she loved him. They were a normal couple in love who spent night after night cuddling their baby—or at least, such normalcy was what they showed to the world. Yet, deep down, he never stopped tormenting himself with the idea that he was nothing but a convenient second choice, who was rewarded year after year with gratitude rather than love. There were some topics which they never discussed, and there were times he wondered if their entire marriage was built on lies. He used to upset himself with thoughts of jealousy and scenarios where the truth would suddenly resurface; but this was long ago. This was before he grew confident and stronger and learned to decompress his worries.

When Bernadette's father retired, Michael took over his dental clinic. He knew she was afraid he had accepted only out of obligation but over the years, it became apparent that Michael loved living in the countryside as much as she did, along with the economic advantages that such a decision brought. The clinic had an excellent reputation and many patients. On top of this, its location was in a building belonging to Bernadette's family. Michael had practically inherited a well-established business, expense-free. As a result, they could invest more in the mortgage to build the house of their dreams. They wanted a private spot, but not too secluded. After a few months of searching, they found what they wanted on the Green Hills, which was nothing but a hilled country land just off the road from the village. It was once a hamlet in the 19th century with its own church, now converted to a private residence and pub. The distance between the Green Hills and the village was minimal. They could easily walk or cycle into town. They were secluded enough but without feeling isolated, as there were neighbouring houses along both sides of the road within a reasonable distance from each other. They bought the land and started building the house of their dreams. Though it was too big for them then, they were planning to add to their family of two. The location was perfect for the couple, and not even the fact that the Flynn's family residence was just a couple of houses further up the road ever spoiled the illusion that they had found their little piece of paradise. And that is exactly how it has been for the last twenty-three years. Admittedly, there were times when Bernadette dreaded the idea of Shane coming back. Even when his parents moved abroad, she never gave that possibility a second thought. It was only when she saw contractors renovating the house that she began to feel uneasy. The gossips in the village later confirmed that Shane was moving back. Upon hearing the news, Bernadette's little castle of cards started to quake.

4

As was his daily routine, Michael parked the Mercedes in his designated parking space in front of the clinic. Before getting out of the car, he took a last look at himself like he did every morning and smiled at his own image. He was in his fifties but felt and looked in better shape than many other younger blokes. When he looked in the mirror, he liked what he saw. He was especially proud of his hair; it was thick, slightly long, and always carefully combed back with the help of some hairstyling wax holding his quiff together. He was an attractive, well-groomed man with money; and money gives one power over women, which he'd discovered first-hand. Doctor Michael Greaney was successful in every aspect of his life; there was no room in his present life for the insecure man he once was, or at least not on the surface. Taking over Bernadette's father's dental practice was the best thing he had ever done. It changed their income and lifestyle since day one, and he would be forever grateful for the opportunity. He had worked hard over the years to expand the business. He owed nothing to anyone, and while he sometimes took pleasure in showing off his money or indulging himself, he felt no shame in doing so. Michael took his briefcase and got out. He aimed his car key remote at the vehicle and waited to hear the beep confirming that his Mercedes SLK—a Christmas present he gave himself the year before—was locked properly. Bernadette never really paid attention to cars or brands, in general; she just bought what she liked, whether it was from the finest boutique in town or a thrift shop. She could do that because she had nothing to prove—she came from money. He didn't, and showing the world his achievements was part of his success.

If Bernadette was hard to impress, Libbie was not! He was old and experienced enough to understand what a woman wanted when she set her eyes on him. Every powerful man has a weakness, and Michael was no exception—his was his ego. With Libbie, he felt chosen. She was young and showered him with praise. She was pure passion; she was the storm while Bernadette was the stillness after it. Was he in love with Libbie? No! Did he have fun with her? Yes! And his ego was highly gratified as much as his body when they were together. It was difficult to give that up. He knew their relationship was going too far, but it was hard to stop. He had tried a couple of times months ago, but there was always a big cry, a desperate plea for one last time. Then, one thing lead to another, and the affair kept going. He'd had a few indiscretions before, but they were all one-night stands or very brief. He usually targeted married women, because they tended to be less complicated and demanding, and would run happily back to their husbands in the end. The story with Libbie didn't start much differently from the others, and it was supposed to end in the same way—they were supposed to return to their respective partners as soon as they had had enough of each other. Unfortunately, Libbie didn't want to go back to her husband, nor did she want to let Michael go. The first time he tried to end the affair, she threw a big scene and cried incessantly, claiming that he was her only reason to live. She told him he was the reason she woke up every morning and fought her abusive, lowlife husband. As a result, Michael agreed to pay her rent for a little flat where she could escape from her unhappy domestic life. Michael thought this would have pacified her and make the breakup easier; Libbie instead saw it as an opportunity to see each other more and without worries. Soon, the flat became their place, where she could play Mrs Greaney.

That day was particularly busy at the clinic. While checking the appointment list, Michael regretfully noticed Tim Warnock's name. Tim was the husband of Bernadette's best friend, Jane. The four of them occasionally went out for dinner or played tennis together, but only for the sake of their wives. Truth to be told, there was an undeclared antipathy between Michael and Tim. To make things worse, one evening, he had told Bernadette he was going to play tennis after work, while he went to Libbie's instead. What he hadn't predicted was that his wife had decided to surprise him by joining him at the tennis club. After all, he was the one always pushing her to be more active. When Bernadette arrived at the club, he was nowhere to be found. Jane and Tim were there too, and they confirmed he had not been playing since they had arrived over an hour prior. Bernadette tried to ring him, but he wasn't answering his phone. Michael only saw the missed calls when he was leaving Libbie's flat, and as soon as he was out of his mistress's earshot, he rang back his wife.

"Hey, honey, sorry I just saw your calls. Is everything okay?" For the first time, Michael felt panic and feared being caught for cheating.

"You tell me—I'm here at the club and have been for over an hour. I thought you were here, and then, when you didn't answer the phone, I got worried."

Michael quickly had to come up with a reasonable explanation for not being where he said he would be. "Everything is fine. I am on my way there. I will explain everything to you once there." When he arrived at the club, Bernadette was at the bar with Tim and Jane. The good old 'I got an emergency call' excuse worked perfectly with Bernadette, but the glance between Tim and Jane showed that it didn't fly with them.

"I thought you had a young doctor for after hours?" Tim enquired. Quick on his feet, Michael answered without flinching, "Well, as the saying goes, 'First come, first served.' The calls are sent to both our phones, and whoever answers first goes." He took a long sip of his Guinness and hoped that his answer would put the matter to rest.

"Strange, because I had to call out of hours before—honey, do you remember that time you told me it was too late to bother a friend for a favour, and you made me call the studio emergency number, but there was only one doctor available on call?" Tim refused to let it go, but Jane kicked him gently under the table. It was not the time or the place. Since then, Michael was under the impression that Tim and Jane saw him differently and suspiciously. Well, it was more than an impression—he knew they had smelled something fishy and were looking forward to discovering dirt they could eventually throw at him. So, he tried to avoid common social engagements, to not give rise to any suspicion in his wife, who seemed oblivious to it all.

While waiting for the next patient, it dawned on Michael that Bernadette might be too oblivious not to notice or mind anything. The other morning, for example, when he left an hour earlier than usual to go to Libbie's, she didn't even bother to ask him why he was leaving for work so early. Was there something going on with her? Did she know about the affair? Or was it simply his paranoid mind playing tricks on him?

5

(THE DAY OF THE FINDING)

The hot water that drizzled on her skin felt good. She leaned on the shower wall and let herself slip slowly to the floor. She brought her knees up to her chest and let the water wash away the tears that streamed incessantly on her face. Bernadette didn't know how long she sat there, but judging by her wrinkly fingertips, it was long enough. She lifted one arm and grabbed the handle of the shower's glass double door to help herself up. She stepped out, put on her bathrobe and opened the window to let the steam out. She wiped the mirror dry. Her eyes were red and puffy. Not even her expensive Elizabeth Arden concealer could miraculously cover the aftermath of her tears. She threw on a pair of yoga pants with a jumper and towel-dried her hair quickly; there was no time for a blow-dry. Michael would be home any minute now. Thankfully, there were some leftovers in the fridge to heat up. She was in no condition to cook tonight, nor did she have the time. She placed the improvised dinner in the oven and chopped some tomatoes and cucumbers. Normally, she would have added some lettuce but she had no time to rinse any. Since Samuel had convinced her to grow her own vegetables, she no longer had handy "ready to use" packs of salad in the house.

"Come on, Mum—there's plenty of space in the garden for a greenhouse. I think it's ridiculous that we keep spending money to buy vegetables from God knows where, when we can grow our own. I'll help." And so, he did. He helped to build the greenhouse at the back of the garden, but then, he went to the States where he quickly traded healthy, home-grown vegetables for the tastier Dunkin Doughnuts pastries, leaving Bernadette taking care of everything. She learned to love her little orchard and took pride in her vegetables and fruits, consisting mainly of strawberries, blueberries, black-berries, raspberries, red berries etc. In Ireland, one can't grow much else but berries. They may be of different shapes and colours, but they were berries nonetheless. The red juice squeezing out the diced tomatoes made Bernadette's mind freeze and brought her back to that afternoon and of the body, the blood, and what she had done—images that will stay with her forever and that no amount of soap and water could ever wash away. The sound of her mobile vibrating on the kitchen counter brought her back to reality, just in time before she cut her index finger in her daze. A notification popped up on the screen, with the words, "Burn your clothes." Then, she remembered the bloodstained clothes she had left on the bath-room floor. The phone slipped off her wet fingers and hit the ground. She dried her hands properly and picked it up. No damage done. Bernadette erased the text message in a frenzy and placed the chopped vegetables in a salad bowl. She dumped the chopping board and the knife in the sink and bolted up the stairs. She didn't have enough time to light a fire and burn the clothes, as Michael had returned home.She stuffed everything in a plastic bag and hid it deep in the laundry basket. She would dispose of it later.

That night, she couldn't sleep. Her head was flooded with thoughts and images of the murder, her hands covered in blood, and Shane's hands all over her aroused body. Every time she closed her eyes, the same scene repeatedly played, featuring two lovers having each other savagely, a shooting and a hooded figure running from the scene.

6

The day was rainy and miserable, and the last thing Bernadette wanted to do was going out, but she had to go. She couldn't keep hiding in the house. During the past week; she'd barely got dressed, and when she ventured a foot outdoors, she returned it promptly with the excuse of feeling unwell. First, it was a headache. Then, it was a migraine. Then, she felt like she was coming down with something. But now, she was running out of excuses. She also wanted her life back. Part of her life consisted of regular trips to the post office to send parcels to Samuel or to return the wrong-sized garments she had purchased online. The latter was precisely the reason she had to go out today. She had a dress in the wrong size sitting in her closet for over three weeks, and today was the last day to send it back. Bernadette typically sent back unwanted items straight away, but with everything that had happened, she'd forgotten about the dress. Since the finding, the villagers talked of nothing else. As the local paper was issued only monthly, the last edition had missed the discovery. Yet, they promptly covered the news on their Facebook page, which had never seen so many hits and likes since its creation. For the most part, the coverage consisted of public opinions and interviews with whoever knew the victim. The local authorities proved to be very good at keeping details from the public even if, among multiple speculations, there was also that it was not a matter of discretion but more the police not having any leads and being nowhere close to solving the case.

Like in most small Irish towns, Seacross's post office was located inside the local convenience store, Maude. Maude was more of a mini-market, where to find nearly everything one needed. Of course, the village also had a proper supermarket, the kind that belonged to a bigger chain, where the villagers did their weekly food shopping. Maude carried daily essentials and some tasty and genuine ready-made food for takeaway. Everybody loved the store's fresh vegetable or chicken soup and their beef stroganoff with roast potatoes. Maude also offered a daily baked variety of Danish pastries, apple crumbles and tarts that tasted as though they were made traditionally by a granny.

As Samuel was no longer living at home with them, Bernadette didn't need to have her pantry filled to feed an army, and so she shopped mainly at Maude's.

That convenience store was a sort of historical place in the village. The elderly would go to the cafe upstairs with their newspaper in hand to read while enjoying a black tea and a warm home-baked scone with cream and jam. The little ones populated Maude on Fridays after school for ice cream or candies, while the teens—with the punctuality of a Swiss clock—gathered together at 1 p.m. to buy their stuffed baguettes before returning to school for their afternoon classes.

Bernadette sometimes liked to go to Maude's cafe alone. Her generation was probably the only one in town not to love and feel the appeal of it. No one could deny it was old-fashioned and in desperate need of refurbishing, but Bernadette loved it nonetheless and found it a place that brought her reassurance and relaxation in some way. It had the power to bring her back in time when her father used to bring her in for their weekly treat. It was just the two of them, usually on Saturdays while her mother had her unmissable weekly appointment at the hairdresser. These days, none of her friends liked going to Maude's. "Honey, the only way you can succeed in bringing me there is if they start boozing their coffee with vodka," Jane always joked. Most people her age went to the deli located opposite Maude's, a fancy place that served the best panini ever.

Unfortunately, "The Gipsy Caravan", as it was called, was also the actual size of a small caravan. The little tables were so close it was impossible not to eavesdrop on the conversation of others. Still, it was there where most of the village's social functions happened and it was where Bernadette went to socialise. Maude's was her "private-public space" as she liked to call it, and where she could go to enjoy solitude and peace, as it was a refuge from all the senseless and boring cheap chats with some acquaintances.

By pure luck, she found parking right in front of the entrance. She removed the parcel from the front passenger seat and ran into the store to spare it from the rain. Much to her annoyance, the queue to the post office was long, and she felt like a slice of ham sandwiched tightly between two terrible slices of bread—two of the most vicious gossipers in the village. In fairness, since the finding, the whole town revealed its natural inclination to gossip and form speculations, not to mention its thirst for gory details, regardless of validity. Police failed to leak any information, which caused disappointment and frustration, eventually resulting in harsh criticism towards the local sergeant still in charge of the investigation.

"See, that's the widow," the lady in front of Bernadette whispered to the woman behind her, and all three pairs of eyes turned towards the entrance and quickly turned back around. Bernadette couldn't say she knew the woman, but her face was somewhat familiar. She tried to remember where she could have met her without success. *Maybe the woman had just a familiar face*, she reasoned. But Bernadette never forgot a face. She was terrible with names, yet faces stayed imprinted in her memory indelibly.

"I never really understood what a woman like that could find in a lowlife like him. The poor man rests in peace now, but he was certainly not a saint." The same woman kept going, "I heard she used to live in London with a rich man who is now doing time for fraud. He allegedly stole funds from his company. The luxury life they had was apparently amazing."

Bernadette was unsure if the woman was talking directly to her or to the lady behind her. When a voice behind her replied, she felt relieved she was not involved in the conversation.

"Oh, so what did she think, that the poor Paul could give her the same lifestyle with his local dealing company? She might be beautiful, but she sure isn't very clever. What you say, Bernadette?" Her luck was over. Before she could even think of something to say, a third woman jumped into the conversation: "Did you know him well, Bernadette? I mean, you must remember him. He was Shane Flynn's best buddy, until the tragedy, of course. I must say, at the time I wasn't sure if

Shane had something to do with it. I mean, he was not a saint either—but look at him now, all rich and successful. Even if I still don't get what it is he does exactly, or how he makes all that money."

"I heard he made his fortune online or through IT; I am not sure. Some company he founded and sold..." the first woman interrupted.

Shane's return, and as a rich man who kept to himself no less, had been another fount of gossip and speculation in the village. It was not as gripping and juicy as a murder, but it was the occasional topic of discussion. For a moment, the three women seemed to have forgotten that Bernadette was standing in front of them, "And the field where they found the body belongs to Flynn. A pretty weird coincidence, is it not?"

Then, they suddenly remembered her existence and turned their attention to her, "You live just a couple of houses away from the scene, don't you?" One of the women who couldn't hide her excitement to have a possible first-hand source in front of her asked, "So, basically, it happened in your back-yard. Oh, my gosh—you poor darling. I could not sleep peacefully after such a tragedy."

Empathy with your suspect to make it talk is the first thing everybody learns watching crime drama.

'Yes, I can't sleep properly after the finding and after what had happened even before the murder. As much as I enjoyed it, body and soul, you are testing my nerves and patience. So, if you don't mind, could you just shut the fuck up and leave me alone?!' Those were the words Bernadette wanted to

speak. The thought of their shocked stupid faces if she had dared to say such things, made her smile.

"I am sorry, ladies, but Shane and I are not close anymore, and I know only about as much as you do. But for your peace of mind, it had happened at a decent distance from my back garden, and I *can* sleep at night," she said instead. Her tone was harsher than she had intended, and her words sharper than she had wanted. The three women stood in embarrassment with their mouths slightly open, speechless for the first time in a long while.

"Sorry, Bernadette. We have been highly indelicate," one of the three replied, after recomposing herself and finding the courage to speak. Bernadette showed her appreciation with a forced smile. Thereafter, in silence, they each waited their turn in the queue. The gossip session was over, at least until Bernadette would be out of their way.

"I'm sure I saw them talking together more than once. I think she knows more than she wishes to say," one whispered. "Talking to who?" said another, "To Shane, obviously. Hello? Are you on this planet today, or not?"

The three women didn't do their best to whisper out of Bernadette's earshot, and she could hear them, even after it was her turn to approach the counter.

After sending off the parcel, she stood by the outside wall of Maude's, oblivious to the pouring rain. Her head was spinning, while her legs felt heavy and were shaking. She leaned on the wall, soaked and in a state of trance as though nothing else existed around her.

"Hey, Bernie. Are you ok?" She looked up and saw Tim standing in front of her. At the touch of his hand on her arm, she shook the stupor off.

"Hey, Tim... yeah, of course. I was just in my little world, you know. I better go now, I'm soaked. I need to take these wet clothes off." She gave him a weak and unconvincing smile and walked to her car.

By the time Bernadette arrived home, her car seat was just as soaked as she was. After she quickly changed into something dry, she went back downstairs for a coffee and some chocolate—that was what she needed. Honeycombs chocolate was the food needed on difficult days. As a dentist, Michael obsessively stressed the importance of flossing to remove the residues on her teeth. She hated flossing, and she hated that he had forever spoiled her chocolate indulgence. Now, every time she gave it a bite, she couldn't help but visualise all the minuscule pieces of food wedged between her teeth. "You're lucky you don't have to floss," Bernadette said to Berta and Pedro.

Once she finished consuming her comfort snack, and while brushing her teeth rigorously, Bernadette suddenly recalled where she had seen Paul's widow. She once saw her leaving the clinic—she was one of Michael's patients.

7

"Oh, my gosh, Shane. You are going to shock that poor girl with all the cologne you have on!"

His mother reached up from her armchair to fix his tie.

"For God's sake, Mery. Leave the boy alone. It's his big night, and every woman loves a well-scented man," said his father.

"You look good, Son. The only reason I don't wear as much cologne nowadays is that your mother will get jealous otherwise," his father continued, while getting up and walking over to his wife to hug her tightly, "Isn't that true, darling?"

Shane could still hear his parents' words in his head. His parents were one of the happiest couples Shane had ever seen. He could only hope that he and Bernadette could share as much love by the time they reached his parents' age. The little blue velvet box was in his jacket, inside the front pocket. He had it all planned; he'd booked a table at the local restaurant, ensuring they would have complete privacy, and when it would be time for desserts, he would give Bernadette the ring. He was nervous and arrived too early, so he decided to drive around. He stopped on the seafront under a lamppost; the sight of the sea always had the power to calm him down. The evening was particularly dark due to bad weather. It was pouring rain, but to the young man in love, it didn't matter. He went through his proposal speech in his mind and imagined Bernadette's reaction, accepting to marry him with a big smile on her face. She would probably blush – she always did when she was the centre of attention – and push her long red hair back, an involuntary habit she had when nervous. They would then toast with their champagne glasses and start planning their life together. But Shane never made that proposal to Bernadette.

Sitting on the prominent corner sofa in his living room, Shane thought about that night, twenty-three years ago. It was the night when his life changed forever. It was impossible not to revisit the past, with everything that had recently happened. He quaffed his whiskey and looked at his phone. Shane knew it was unsafe to call her and she'd said she didn't want to see him again. Still, now that he'd found her again, he had no intention of letting her go, but this time, he wanted an explanation. She owed it to him. The sleeping pills he took started to take their effect, facilitated by the alcohol. He threw his head back, closed his eyes, and the past came alive again in his dreams where he heard the words, 'He confessed everything, and all the charges have been dropped.' He will never forget that phone call from his sister. He could have his life back and Bernadette. He was standing by the phone in the hall of his Viennese flat and had to grab a chair and sit. He was free to go back, free to use his real name, free to see his family. Free to see Bernadette again.

"What about Bernie?" he asked immediately.

"She is gone, Shane. She didn't stick around to wait for you. Forget her."

He couldn't believe she had not waited for him. She hadn't believed in his own innocence and disappeared from his life. Years passed, life went on, and Shane never returned to Seacross. His father retired shortly after Shane moved to Vienna, and with his wife, they decided to move to Malaga to be closer to their daughter, Clarisse. After their parents died, the only thing that linked the siblings to Seacross was their old family home. Neither of them had any interest in the house, until now. Clarisse and Shane had always been close, and even more once the two of them were the only left of their family. If Shane was back, it was due to his sister.

8

There is no delicate or easy way to tell someone they are dying. Over the months, Dr Carvellas had grown fond of his Irish patient. She was a fighter, but unfortunately, her will to fight the enemy that was slowly consuming her was not enough. They tried everything they could to help her. Yet, the reality was they were now out of alternatives.

"How long are we talking about?" Clarisse asked with a tired but firm voice.

"It is hard to say precisely how much time, Clarisse, but I would say no more than three or four months. We might hope for five if you agree to the experimental treatments here in the hospital. I have already told you about this new American therapy," Clarisse raised her hand to make him stop talking.

"No, I think that is enough, doctor. I am too tired and I'm dying anyway. Three months, four months, five months—what difference do they make? I'm tired of hospitals and treatments, and I want to spend the last few months of my life with dignity. I want to die in my own home and on my own terms."

When she left the hospital, she expected to feel sad and devastated. Instead, she just felt tired. She was tired of fighting a battle that was impossible to win and tired of lying to everyone around her. Sometimes, she wondered what was consuming her: was it the cancer, or the secret she was carrying? When she had sworn to keep it, she was young and had never thought of its implications. But over the years, she realised what it had meant for her brother and her parents, and the remorse she had in keeping that secret from them never abandoned her. She kept her word all these years, but now things were different. There was now a way to ease her conscience without having to break her word. Shane was due to visit her in a month and by then, everything should have been organised and ready.

"You should go back home" she told him one night. "I think it's time you faced the past, or you can never move on with your life." Clarisse's words took Shane entirely by surprise. She kissed him on the cheek and went to bed.

The following morning, Shane woke up at six-thirty to go running before it got too hot outside. He ran his usual route, stopped to stretch and returned home to shower before breakfast. When he arrived, Merce the housekeeper was unloading the dishwasher, while Clarisse was still in bed. When Clarisse had not awoken by ten o'clock, Shane knocked on her bedroom door, but there was no answer.

"Merce, have you seen if Miss Clarisse has gone out?" he asked.

"No, *Señor* Shane," Merce replied with her strong accent. Clarisse had seemed especially down and frail in the last few days, and this raised some concerns in her brother who called for her one more time from outside the door before he carefully turned the handle.

"Come on, sleeping beauty. It's getting late," Shane said, while drawing the curtains after he saw his sister was still under the covers.

The Clarisse he knew would have covered her eyes, complained and would probably have thrown a pillow at him in protest. Since they were kids, he had always been an early riser, while she was more of a night owl. He turned around, expecting to see her long and slim limbs stretching out from underneath the covers; instead, she was laying still. With the light now illuminating the room, he saw an empty bottle of pills on the bedside table. Shane rushed to the bed, dropped to his knees and shouted at his sister to wake up while shaking her lifeless body vigorously.

"What have you have done? What have you done?" he repeated softly like a mantra, while an uncontrollable flow of tears ran down his face. He didn't understand why she had done such a thing. If there was one person who was in love with life, it was his sister. Merce was standing by the door, with her right hand glued to her mouth as she tried to silence her sobs. In her left hand was a letter.

Merce eventually found the courage to step into the room. She kneeled beside a desperate Shane. "She was very sick. She didn't want anybody to know..."

As the housekeeper related the account of Clarisse's last year of life, every word hit Shane like stubs. How could he have missed it? What kind of brother was he? As Merce knew what he was thinking, she touched his shoulder delicately. She removed his hands from his face, which he had covered in desperation and shame. "It is not your fault," she whispered as she tried to console him. Shane lifted his face and got up, pulling Merce off him. Pain and rage mixed inside him.

"How would you know? What do you know?" he shouted angrily at the poor maid and left the bedroom. Merce put away the envelope in the front pocket of her apron and followed Shane on the balcony. They stood next to each other, with their hands tightly gripping the railing while staring quietly at the sea. Both their faces were wet with tears. They stayed there in silence for a while. "I am sorry, Merce. I didn't want to take it out on you, but I don't understand. Why hadn't she told me anything? Why didn't she confide in me? Why didn't she trust me?", Merce pulled out two chairs for them to sit.

"She trusted you more than anybody else, but she didn't want you to suffer along with her. The last check-up was bad. She was told she only had a few months left, and she didn't want to spend them in the hospital. She wanted to die in her own home and on her terms, with dignity." Merce got up, and while she gave Shane a sympathetic pat on his hands, she removed the envelope from her apron and handed it to him. It was a plain white and ordinary envelope, with only his name written on the back in Clarisse's unmistakable handwriting.

9

The return flight from Malaga to Vienna was packed with noisy students. Shane put on his earphones and mentally revisited Clarisse's funeral. Only a dozen people attended. He thought it weird that she didn't have many friends despite having lived there for so long. The letter Merce gave him was a puzzle his sister had left to solve. Why was she so adamant for him to return to Seacross? What did she mean by, 'Once there, you will understand'? Shane tried not to think about it too much, all these questions were probably destined to remain unanswered anyway. But admittedly, the words had planted seeds in his head. Even after returning to his life in Vienna, he could not stop thinking about his sister's last words to him.

Shane usually went to Spain for Christmas and spent the holidays with Clarisse. This year, however, there was no Clarisse, and he was on his own. Friends had offered to have him over, but he would have felt like an intruder in someone else's family, in someone else's life. The truth was that this year, he had nowhere to go for Christmas; except back home to

Ireland. Apart from the multitude of newly built residential estates everywhere inland, nothing had changed around Seacross. Shane decided to stay in a B&B outside the village. After all those years of vacancy, his parents' house was not fit to be inhabited. Yet, that was not the only reason he had decided to stay elsewhere. He didn't want to be seen around; until he had decided what to do. Shane parked outside Paul's apartment block. He knew Paul had been released from prison and had moved back home with a wife. He had the one thing he took away from him. When Shane saw Paul leaving the building, he unknowingly clenched his two fists so tight that his fingers nails left a deep mark on his palms. Shane drove away and stopped at the first convenience store where he felt it was safe to shop without the risk of being recognised. He bought a bottle of vodka for self-medication and forgot the betrayal that had ruined his life. The trip back to Seacross had been more emotionally painful than he had expected.

On his last day before returning to Vienna, he had a drive through the village. He didn't want to arrive at the airport too early, and told himself that it was a good way to waste some time before heading off. The truth was that he hoped to see Bernadette. If the purpose of this trip was to face his past, he had to do so fully. He knew she had moved back to the village too, with her husband and son. Shane didn't know how he would react if he ever saw her again. In a way, he dreaded the encounter but at the same time, he wished for it. Shane had nearly lost all hope when he stopped at the pedestrian crossing. The rain was heavy, resulting in condensation on his windshield. He doubted that anybody could see inside his car, meanwhile he had a perfect view of who was crossing the road. He could recognise that walk anywhere. The rain hat and the long coat were not enough to disguise her. He followed her until she went into the hair salon. He pulled over just outside and waited for her to remove her coat and take a seat. Like the village, even Bernadette had not changed that much over the years. She was slightly more substantial than he remembered, and her red hair was not as long anymore. It was just past her neck now, but still curly and wild. She was still beautiful, but she was not his Bernie anymore. She didn't wait for him, and she didn't give him a second chance. He still didn't know why, but now he knew what he had to do. He had to come back. He never felt at home in Vienna, anyway. He had arrived there as a fugitive. Even after Paul confessed to the crime, and all charges had been dropped against him, he still felt out of place. Unfortunately, Seacross didn't feel like home either; and for the last twenty-three years, he never returned because of the shame and stigma he still felt. Never mind that his name was cleared; he was now an innocent man who lost his life. Becoming a successful and wealthy businessman didn't take away his sense of precariousness. He'd never made peace with his past, and maybe that was what Clarisse meant with her words. He had to face his ghosts and eventually have closure with his past, which for too long had prevented him from living his present and planning his future.

10

"Wouldn't it be better to take two shirts instead of only one? And two pairs of trousers? You know, just in case you spill some wine on you. I also added a cardigan. Evenings are getting colder."

"Dear Lord, Bernadette, I'm going to a bloody golf weekend with a bunch of old goats – I don't think I'll be required to dress up formally for dinner," Michael snapped at his wife from the bathroom.

"Oh, well—OK. No need to get so snappy!" Bernadette zipped closed Michael's bag.

"Just add your toothbrush in the front pocket, then," she coldly added, leaving the room.

Michael spat the mouthwash in the sink and dried his mouth. He knew he had no reason to snap, but he was going away with Libbie for the first time for an entire weekend. He was nervous. He was afraid of getting caught, and he also feared that this weekend in Wicklow, which Libbie had suggested, would be the first of many. She made it clear to him that now that she was a free woman, she would never let him go, and he no longer had any aces up his sleeves. He couldn't threaten to reveal everything to Paul anymore, as if she ever cared.

"Now, my dear, I'm sorry your plan didn't work, as my useless husband managed to get himself murdered first. There's not much you can use against me now, is there? I may be a free woman now, but I can still open my mouth and tell your wife about us. I know you said you were ready to come clean for the sake of your marriage, but how do you think she will react when she discovers that I am only the last one of a long series of women?" Her words ended Michael's last attempt to end his affair with Libbie. He was trapped again. Libbie was right; it was one thing to confess to an affair, but it would be entirely another if his wife were to discover he was a serial cheater. Bernadette owed him and probably still felt indebted to him – after all, he had agreed to keep her secret and be her accomplice, but what he knew was insufficient to save his marriage should his unfaithfulness be discovered. Bernadette's secret was also his secret now and revealing it would destroy their family. After that conversation, Michael had not heard from Libbie for a few days, but he didn't expect it was because she had decided to let him go. On the contrary, he knew she was plotting something. He was right in his assumption, as Libbie eventually rang, "I've had a few stressful weeks, and I could do with a week away," she said, "I saw a nice spa hotel in Wicklow where we could go…" As she trailed on, he tuned her out.

That same evening, Libbie sent him a text with the reservation she had made under the name of Mr and Mrs Greaney. It was clear to him that she would be the one to decide when their story ends. She was out of control, and he had no other choice but to find a believable excuse to go away on his own over the weekend. Bernadette didn't play golf and had no interest in it, so telling her that he was going away with his golfing pals for the weekend would not have arisen any suspicion or questions. The only problem could be Tim Warnock, as he played in the same club. Michael only hoped that Bernadette would not mention the trip to Jane, and to ensure she wouldn't, he told her Tim had been invited too but couldn't go. There was still a chance Bernadette could talk about the trip with Jane or Tim, but it was a risk he had to take.

11

"You need to fix the light at the gate. I couldn't even see the bell in the dark. By the way, here—this is for you, hon. It'll go perfectly with this homemade pavlova." Jane blew into Bernadette's kitchen. After she disposed of the bag containing the goodies she had bought, she gave her friend a big long hug. While Jane made herself comfortable on one of the chairs by the counter, Bernadette lifted the cake cover and swiped the side of the cake with her index finger, "Mmm," she groaned as she licked the icing on her upper lip, "God bless Tim's mother."

"Well, could it not have been me who baked it this time?" Jane said, feigning an outraged and offended look.

"Of course… not!" Bernadette answered, as she took another swipe of icing and kissed Jane on her forehead, who was still giggling.

"I'd better put it in the fridge, or I'll eat it all before dinner. So, what were you saying about the gate? Something about the lamp outside not working and you can't see a bloody thing in the dark? "

"Yes, your gate lamp is not working"

"Ah, that damned gate. I don't know. This morning, it was the remote and now, it's the lamp. I'll ask Michael to have a look at it when he is back." Bernadette was particularly happy to have Jane over. More than ever, she needed her friend. If only she could tell her everything. Maybe she would, someday. Lately, she often thought about spilling everything to Jane, but she was afraid of her reaction, and might lose her.

"Mmm, it smells nice! What are you cooking in there? Let me guess. Your best friend's favourite: your amazing American chicken casserole?!" Bernadette smiled and opened the oven for a second to show Jane the casserole inside.

When in Uni, Bernadette shared the room briefly with an American girl who passed onto her mother's chicken casserole recipe. Jane loved Bernadette's American chicken casserole and so did Bernadette; over the years, it became her favourite dish to cook at home. The only problem was that the long wild rice required for the recipe was impossible to find in Ireland. Now that Samuel was living in Boston, he shipped boxes of it regularly to his mother.

Jane opened the wine and poured two glasses.

"Aren't you driving, naughty girl?" Bernadette asked, as Jane had arrived in her own car.

"Only on my way here, dear. I'm planning to leave my car with you overnight and collect it tomorrow."

"As long as you pay for the parking, it's fine by me," Bernadette said cheekily before lifting her glass and making a toast.

When the oven's timer finally rang, the two women had already drunk a full bottle, and they were desperate to fill their stomachs. After having a second bottle with the casse-role, they were both stuffed but refused to pass on some sherry and a slice of pavlova. It was getting late; the alcohol was kicking in, and when the yawns started to interrupt the conversation too often, the two friends decided to call it a night. Jane phoned for a taxi.

"Come on, madam! I'll be sure to get you home safely or who is going to hear that temperamental husband of yours," said the taxi driver, a local man they both knew from their school days. Halfway down the driveway, the taxi stopped and the driver's window rolled down, "Hey Bernie, you must do something with that gate lamp, I couldn't even see the bell."

"See? I told you!" added Jane, whose head stuck out from the other window, before blowing her a kiss as the taxi drove off. Bernadette waved as the car left and went back inside. *Bernie*, she thought. Nobody called her that since she was a teen except Shane, and Frank, obviously. She let the dogs out, and when they were done and back inside, she locked the doors and windows. She set the alarm, and after switching all the lights off, went upstairs. Michael was obsessed with leaving some lights on at night, but she thought it was a waste of energy. With extreme effort, she undressed, and without bothering to remove the makeup still on her face, crashed on the bed. She hadn't realised how drunk she was until she laid her head on the pillow and everything started to spin around her. She hated that feeling, but was so tired that it took only a few minutes before she was sound asleep.

The morning light was peeking through the curtains. With one eye open, Bernadette checked the time. Her head was still heavy and her stomach sluggish. She went to the windows to pull the curtains and see the weather outside. It was cloudy – the perfect weather to have a lay-in day. Pedro and Berta had slept beside her on the bed. Normally, they would have slept on the floor at the feet of the bed, but as the master was not home, they must have felt entitled to use the free space next to her. They looked at her with lazy eyes and yawned. When Bernadette threw on her old cashmere cardigan, too worn out to be used outside but still soft and warm, the two dogs got up too, and the three of them went straight into the kitchen. Bernadette was dying for a black coffee, and with only that in mind, she opened the garden door to let the dogs out, forgetting she had not unset the alarm before doing so. She covered her ears immediately to stop the noise from puncturing her eardrums and ran into the hall where the alarm box was. The landline rang shortly after she deactivated the alarm. It was the police. She initially thought they were calling regarding her involvement in the finding and her first reaction was fear, until she realised it was nothing but the routine call whenever the alarm triggered. She answered the security questions, and once the guards were convinced she had set the alarm off by mistake, they hung up. The percolator was filled with the sweet scent of brewed coffee, and Bernadette poured herself a full mug before switching on the TV. Morning TV was crap enough during the week, but it was even worse over the weekend. She zapped until she found the news channel and raised the volume, as Pedro and Berta devoured their breakfast wildly and loudly. Rather than two Labradors, they sounded like two grinders at full speed. She switched on her mobile. Text alerts covered the screen. She had a few texts from Jane, thanking her for the evening, reminding her how much she loved her and how much of a pain it would have been assisting Tim's tennis match in a hangover. There was also a text from Michael saying he will ring once he was done and ready to leave. Then, there were uncountable texts and voicemails from Shane. He wanted to talk; she didn't. She knew she could not keep ignoring him, but she was too afraid of her feelings and his questions. She had made a decision many years ago and telling the truth now would only lead to devastating consequences for far too many people. If only she had the courage to confide in Jane, she could help her as she always had, but the fear that she would reject and disown her as a friend proved too strong. She was alone in this situation.

12

(THE DAY OF THE FINDING)

They were playing cat and mouse since his return. Shane still had power over her. She knew she shouldn't have accepted the invitation to go to his house, but the truth was that she wanted to go. She craved for him, and she knew they would be together the moment she rang the bell. Taking advantage of the beautiful day, they had coffee in the garden, but this was different from their encounters at Maude's. They both knew they were venturing down a one-way road from where it would be impossible to return. "Why didn't you wait for me?" asked Shane, his eyes fixed on her. She feared that question for so long; still, she could not tell him the truth, "You left and never got in touch with me. I thought you had made a new life for yourself," Bernadette tried to be convincing, but all she wanted was for him to stop asking questions so she wouldn't have to answer with more lies.

"You know I couldn't stay after what happened that night. The police were after me. I would have ended up in prison, and keeping in touch with you was too risky for both of us. I didn't want you involved in that mess. I was trying to protect you," he explained. "and then, when I was acquitted of all charges, you were already gone." Shane's eyes were filled with sadness and rage. Bernadette lowered hers. She didn't know what to say; she wanted to hug him and tell him everything—the whole truth—but she couldn't bring herself to, as the fear of losing him again was too strong.

"We should leave the past in the past. It is too late now, anyway," she said instead, before standing up and returning inside the house. She didn't want to leave, but she had to hide her tear-covered face from him. Bernadette had one hand on the doorknob already when Shane reached for her and delicately moved her away from the door, pulling her toward him. She didn't fight back, and let her long-lost lover hug her. She didn't dare to move. She was afraid to wake up and discover it had all been a dream. "If you didn't want this as much as I do, you wouldn't be here today," he whispered into her ears before kissing her neck. He was right. Bernadette threw her arms around his neck and kissed him.

13

(THE DAY OF THE FINDING)

For the first time after many years of marriage, she was lying beside a man who was not her husband. Her head rested on Shane's chest while he caressed her back, counting the rings of her spine. She had always liked how he did that; it relaxed and aroused her at the same time. He had not forgotten. She didn't feel bad for letting another man inside her, and it was not because things with Michael were poor intimately as of late, but because it was Shane—her Shane. He was there before her husband. He was her first love, probably her only real love. She felt guilty, not for cheating, but for being happy. It was like nothing existed outside that room. The only reality that mattered in that moment was the two of them being together. She knew it was wrong, but she could not help her feelings for him. Bernadette's mobile rang and reminded the two lovers there was an outside world after all.

"You want to see who it is?" asked Shane, with his arm already reaching out to get the phone from the floor; it likely dropped out of the back pocket of her jeans when he took them off her. Bernadette felt embarrassed. She wondered if it was Michael and she had to call him back. She glanced at Shane, who smiled at her before kissing her forehead. She stopped his arm from getting it. "I'll check later. I'm sure it's nothing important." It probably wasn't, but it did spoil their moment and they had to face reality. Bernadette left the bed first, walking off just as she was without sheets or anything covering her naked body, which featured all the marks from the last twenty-three years of her life. She wondered what Shane thought – was he disgusted by her stretch marks or by her waistline that was now far too round? While she passed his side of the bed to collect her underwear from the floor, he grabbed her free hand and sat her beside him for a moment. His face was still gorgeous, and the deep wrinkles marked by age only gave him more charm. She bent over to kiss him before walking to the bathroom, closing the door behind her. When she returned to the bedroom, Shane had retrieved all her clothes and laid them on the bed. She grabbed her top and covered herself clumsily, as the bathroom mirror showed more signs of her ageing than she would have liked.

"You don't have to cover yourself. You are beautiful. You are still my beautiful Bernie," Shane uttered, standing naked in front of her.

'And you are still my handsome boy,' Bernadette wished she could reply. Instead, she stood there without moving or talking. He got closer and kissed her. She could feel his manhood pushing against her while his hands rested on her breast. He was ready to make love to her again, and so was she. It was getting late, and the daylight outside was starting to fade.

"I have to go now," said Bernadette as she stepped out of bed and started to dress. Shane followed and went straight to the bathroom. She could hear the shower water running and him singing. She was ready to go but was waiting for Shane to return to the room. She didn't want to leave without seeing him one last time and saying goodbye. While waiting, Bernadette opened the French door to the balcony. The view from Shane's bedroom was spectacular. His house was further up the hill and gave him a view of all the fields, which stretched out to the sea, his perspective further enhanced by the telescope sitting on the terrace. She adjusted it to her height and subconsciously aimed it to the far left to see if her garden was visible from where she stood. The high trees made it impossible to see in her property, leaving her to wonder if she felt more protected or disappointed in some way that Shane could not spy on her, just the idea left her feeling thrilled and guilty.

14

Paul had always known Libbie never loved him. She loved the money he made and didn't care it was dirty. Things were great in the beginning, and he even thought she could genuinely fall for him. But he ruined everything, as usual. He had lost control of his vices, and after he was caught drunk on the ferry back from London with all the merchandise on him, he was gradually cut off the business. He was assigned small jobs that even a high-school boy could handle. Money started coming in short until he was no longer able to meet his wife's expectations. When they first met, Libbie assumed he was a big fish in the pond, and Paul did not dissuade her in this belief. Unfortunately, when they moved to Ireland, they each discovered the other's true nature. She was greedy, and he was a loser. It was a match destined to explode sooner or later. Paul knew his wife despised him and was seeing someone else, but he never thought Libbie would move out. She had been excellent at keeping the identity of her secret lover. He hated the way people in the village looked at him with pity and disdain, and even some pleasure as most have never really forgiven him for what he had done that night some twenty-three years ago. The village was small, and he will always be known as the one who robbed and killed an innocent family man while framing his best friend for the murder. Sometimes, he wondered why he even decided to go back to Seacross. The answer was simple; his parents' free house was the only place where he could live. After the trial, Paul's parents didn't want anything to do with him and ensured the village knew how shameful they felt about their son's actions by never speaking to him until they died. Being an only child, he nevertheless inherited their house and some money. The house was a big and detached property that was well-maintained; it was the perfect home to bring Libbie, his new wife. However, it wasn't long before he could no longer keep the house and had to sell it and downsize to a flat in one of the new apartment blocks built during the economic boom which had devaluated gradually over the years. These days, Paul's only company and comfort was the bottle and Dr Phil. Every morning, he woke up and poured himself a mug of coffee, with a cup of cheap whiskey, and sat in front of the TV with the curtains still closed; as a matter of fact, they were permanently closed. He liked Dr Phil. "The man knows his shit," he would always say to Libbie when she would tease him about watching a typical show for desperate housewives. He missed her bitter sarcasm that used to upset him so much. He wished he could still hear her nasty comments, at least someone was still talking to him then. Now, there was just silence. That morning, while sitting in his chair in front of the TV, Paul wondered what Dr Phil would have said to him if he was on one of his shows. '*Have a drink, man. What else do you have left? You are such a loser, and you will never change*,' he imagined Dr Phil saying. With that thought in mind, he stood up and walked to the kitchen cupboard to get a bottle of something. The shelf was desolate, aside from a nearly empty bottle of Jemison whiskey. He unscrewed the tap and drank the last few drops straight from the bottle. He threw it on the ground, went to the bedroom, put on a tracksuit and left. He couldn't remember where he had parked the car the previous night. Somewhere on the strand road probably. There was no point in getting the car; he could just walk to Maude's. He smoked a couple of cigarettes, and when the church bells started to ring at noon sharp, he entered the store and bought two bottles of cheap Cork Dry Gin. With his head down and the two bottles in the brown paper bag, he left the shop.

"Hey, be careful man," said a man whose arm hit his roughly. He was coming in, but it was only when Paul raised his eyes that he saw who the man was. It was Shane Flynn. Paul's jaw dropped; he didn't know what to do, and he didn't know if Shane hit him on purpose. *Did Shane see him?* Paul was so confused and the only thing he wanted at that moment was to unscrew one of the bottles and get drunk so he would not have to think anymore. Paul knew Shane was back and had seen him in town a few times over the months, but being the coward he was, he always avoided crossing paths with him. But this time, it was not possible. Shane made things easy for him by not stopping; he just walked past him and disappeared inside the store. Once outside, Paul looked at his own reflection in the window, and the image of him in a dirty tracksuit with scrappy hair and an unshaved, sleep-deprived face disgusted him. He desperately wanted to go home and drink himself unconscious. As Paul was about to leave for home, Shane came out of the store and was surprised to see his once best friend, who had betrayed and ruined him. Much to Paul's surprise, Shane looked him straight in the eye this time, before passing by him.

"Shane, wait! Please!" It took all the courage Paul had inside him to utter the words.

Shane turned, his eyes were as cold as ice, while simultaneously showing burning fury. "I'm sorry, I don't know you."

At this point, Paul had nothing left to lose and grabbed him by the arm, hoping to get a reaction. Even receiving a punch would be better than being ignored.

"You are dead to me," Shane went on. No matter how hard he tried to keep his voice under control, he had raised his tone, and the people on the street turned to the sound of his words. Shane freed his arm and walked away. Neither man realised that outside the Garda station, Sgt McCabe was standing and watching them from the other side of the road.

Once home, Paul drank himself to sleep on his recliner in front of the TV. When he woke up, he had no idea what time it was. It was mid-to late afternoon, he guessed. His bladder was exploding, and he reached the bathroom just in time. Once he was back in the living room, he lit a cigarette and poured himself a glass of water; his mouth was dry and his breath stale. His mobile buzzed. He checked it immediately, hoping it was some job alert. He could do with some money. It was a brief text message from an unknown number: "I want to meet. We need to talk." He immediately thought it was Libbie. Since she moved out, he had not heard from her; maybe there was still hope, perhaps she wanted to go back home. Maybe Mr X was now fed up with paying her bills. A second text came in with a time and a place. Paul was now sure who it was. Although he was disappointed the text was not from Libbie, a smile appeared on his face. His chance to explain himself and make amends with the past has finally arrived.

15

Paul didn't have much time to get ready. He stank of booze and cigarettes and the shirt he was wearing saw better and cleaner days. He rose from the chair and nearly tripped on the empty bottles at his feet on his way to the shower. After putting on his last clean T-shirt and a used pair of jeans without any visible stains on them, Paul made himself a robust instant black coffee. Libbie took the expensive coffee machine she had made him buy her for Christmas the previous year. He had to admit the thing was worth the money he had spent. He thought about how she was probably making a fancy latte or a cappuccino for her lover right then, after shagging him. His head ached, and his vision was blurry. Paul took a couple of aspirins and grabbed the car keys; there was no way he was going to walk up the Green Hills. "Fuck," he said out loud to no one with a slightly loud tone that made the elderly couple who were passing him turn to look at him. They exchanged a common disapproving look with a young mother who was walking by, who had instinctively covered her son's ears upon hearing him utter the curse.

"What, because you are all pleased when you get a ticket, are you? Fucking hypocrites," he said, as he took the piece of paper from the windshield and waved it in front of them. Still muttering, he got into the car, and after putting the ticket in the glove compartment with the rest of his collection, he drove off. He pulled over to the side of the road a few meters from the entrance of the house. The secret passage to the backyard was still there, the same one they had used when they were young and happy-go-lucky and wanted to remain unseen. Nothing had changed there. The big tree where they used to hang out was still there, except where there used to be two swinging tyres hanging from a branch, there was now just leftover pieces of rope. Paul stood in the middle of the field. The sun was hot and bright. Paul's phone started to vibrate in his pocket, "Hello—yes, I am here. Where are you?" His tone betrayed the excitement he felt for the meeting. He turned, with full expectation of seeing his old friend and begging for his forgiveness. A figure came out from the bushes. Paul took a step closer and said, "Hey, man. I am so happy you called. This means…" Paul stopped when he realised that this figure was not there to make amends. "What the hell..." uttered Paul. He didn't get the chance to beg for forgiveness like he had wanted. Instead, he begged for his life. A slightly shaking arm raised a handgun and aimed it at his chest. Paul automatically brought his hands to the open wound to keep the blood from squirting outside his body. He tried to move and wanted to run, but the pain was too much. He fell to the ground, where the second shot took away every pain from his life, forever.

16

(THE DAY OF THE FINDING)

Bernadette replaced the telescope's position to how it was before she played with it. She was about to return inside when someone walking in the field captured her attention. That was private property, and only a few people knew the shortcut through the main road. She called for Shane, but he was still in the bathroom and couldn't hear her. Curiosity overtook her and she aimed the telescope to watch and follow the figure. Based on the person's build, he could have been anyone, and she couldn't see his face, as an oversized baseball cap covered it. He walked further toward the house and then stopped to check the time like he was waiting for someone. Bernadette started to get cold out there on the balcony, but her curiosity to see what would happen next kept her behind the lens. She thought to call for Shane again but was afraid of being heard by the figure, although the distance was safe enough for her to remain unnoticed. The man extracted something from the pocket of his trousers. His phone was ringing. He answered and started walking toward the wooded side of the field. A second person came out of the woods, wearing a dark hoody and sunglasses that made even gender identification impossible. From there, everything happened so fast that Bernadette couldn't even register what she had just witnessed. The hooded figure had aimed his arm, and then there was a loud, vibrant noise of gunshots. Instinctively, Bernadette pulled away from the telescope. In complete disbelief of what had just happened in front of her eyes and shaking from the shock, she bent and peered into the lens again. The shooter disappeared back into the woods, leaving the other man lying still on the ground.Shane had just stepped back into the bedroom when he heard Bernadette screaming hysterically. Her words made no sense, but when he eventually looked into the telescope, everything was clear.

"What do we do now? We can't leave him there. What if he's still alive? What if the shooter saw me?" spewed Bernadette in a series of questions, on the verge of a panic attack. Shane held her by the shoulders with both hands and shook her gently but vigorously to calm her down.

"Ok, let's focus," he said with authority, although he was panicking as much as she was. Shane was also suffering the same level of shock—or possibly even worse, as he knew far too well the implications of being involved in a murder and had no intention of being associated with another. They went down to the field. The man was not moving, but the biggest shock came when they turned his face toward them. It was Paul Mulligan. Shane turned white as though all the blood had drained from his face. He froze, incapable of moving or talking. Bernadette kneeled to check if there was still a pulse.

"I can't feel anything, but I don't know," She was not in the right mental state to do anything rationally, and neither was

Shane. He kneeled with her and put two fingers under Paul's nose to see if he could feel air in the nostrils.

"I think he is dead," notified Shane.

"We need to call the police," replied Bernie immediately, as she stood up.

"And say what, Bernie? I wished him dead yesterday in town for everyone to hear, and today, he shows up dead in my back garden! What do you think the police will think? They will conclude I killed him out of revenge," Shane reasoned. He could not believe this was happening to him again.

"But you didn't, Shane. I saw what happened."

"And to relate what you saw, you'd have to confess cheating on your husband publicly. Are you ready to do that, Bernie?"

Bernadette's jaw dropped. She hadn't thought about Michael, and worse, she had not thought about Samuel, either. There was no way she could go public with such scandalous information.

"And even if you go to the police and tell them what happened, do you think they will believe you? You are a cheater and liar in their eyes, so how would they know you're telling the truth? Not to mention that Paul ruined your life, too. You could have had the same motive of revenge like me. They will only see you as my accomplice." Shane's words were hard to digest, but they sounded true. Bernadette's legs couldn't keep her standing anymore. She collapsed to the ground, hiding her face in her hands. Maybe this was her punishment for adultery. Shane kneeled and forced her to face him. She had blood everywhere on her, transferred from Paul's body when she checked his pulse.

"Listen to me, Bernie. Now, you go home and clean yourself up. You were never here today, and you haven't seen anything, OK?" Shane waited for her to nod with her head before continuing, "We can't tell the police what we know. This is bad enough for me. Paul and I had a history, and now, he was murdered on my property. They will come knocking at my door, anyway, but I can't be involved in this any more than I already am. The police will most likely come to you too because you are my closest neighbour. We are together in this, and we need to stick to the same story."

Bernadette's head was about to explode. Her romantic afternoon had turned into a gruesome murder case. She was nothing but a liar and a cheater, and the life she had built was now a joke. Suddenly, it was all too much, and she was scared as she had ever been, "We can't see each other again. I'm married, Shane, to another man. What happened today was a mistake." Bernadette didn't sound convincing, not even to herself. She wasn't even sure why she said those words, maybe out of guilt, fear or cowardice.

"Come on, Bernie. Don't give me that. Don't tell me you don't feel anything for me anymore. Don't tell me this afternoon meant nothing to you."

"It doesn't matter what I feel, Shane. It's too late for us now," Bernadette turned her back to him and started to walk home. She wanted to run, but her legs were too heavy, as was her soul. She knew Shane was still the man she wanted.

"Too late," she kept repeating to herself. Suddenly, she felt the highest sense of shame she had ever thought possible. How could she think about love and passion when a man had just been shot in front of her? She was a horrible person, but she still couldn't stop thinking about how pleasant Shane's skin felt on hers once again. She subconsciously touched her face, thinking of Shane's hands touching it gently. But when she saw the blood on her hands and now on her face, she was brought back to reality.

17

For Shane, seeing Paul and talking to him that day brought everything back to his mind and reopened a wound that had never really healed. The image of the Garda car outside his parents' house was still so vivid in Shane's memory: the knock at the door, and the voices of the guards as they searched his home and car. The smell of the interrogation room would stay with him forever. It was nothing like what one sees in movies. It was just a small storage room with a wooden table and three chairs. Sgt McCabe Sr questioned him for hours, and in the end, he let him go home under his parents' responsibility. Seacross's Garda station was, and still is, on the main street, which had made it impossible for the other villagers to miss the show of him being held in handcuffs.

"Jim, you've got to help us here. There must be something we can do," Shane's father pleaded on the phone with the lawyer as soon as they arrived home.

Shane locked himself in the bedroom. He still couldn't believe Paul had turned against him. No matter how many times Shane related what had really happened, the fact remained that the car was still his and the gun had his fingerprints on, not Paul's. Paul premeditated everything, and he had worn gloves. Mr Wilson, the owner of the convenience store, died in the ambulance, and now it was just Shane's word against Paul's, except the evidence pointed only to him as the suspect.Shane now hated him more than anyone else in his entire life. Maybe if he had listened to his lawyer's advice and pleaded guilty, things would have been simpler; he wouldn't have had to run away, and he would not have lost Bernadette in the process. But he was not guilty and refused to confess for a murder he didn't commit.

"I can't plead guilty for something I didn't do," he told his father plainly. For the first time in his life, he questioned his father's authority.

"Don't be a stupid, son. They will charge you for murder. There will be no house arrests; they'll keep you in jail until the trial, and in a proper jail. Montjoy, most likely. Jim has spoken with the district attorney today, they are confident that with the proof the police have on you, the jury will deem you guilty. Of course, with a confession, it will make their job easier. If you confess, they will be ready to cut a deal and reduce your sentence. You'll still be young enough to live your life after you get out of prison. With good behaviour, you can easily get out and only do half your time." His father's words felt like a stab in the back. His own father doubted his innocence; otherwise, he would have never asked him to confess a crime he had never committed. That same night, Clarisse went to his bedroom. "Grab a few things," she said. "I am dropping you at the train station." At first, Shane didn't understand what she was saying. "What are you talking about? I can't go anywhere," he said. But Clarisse had a plan,"You can't stay, either. Otherwise, you'll go to prison."

Shane was incredulous with her suggestion. "So, you want me to become a fugitive on top of being a killer?"

"You are not a killer. And yes—I would rather have you be a fugitive than a convicted criminal for something you haven't done." Clarisse showed him a piece of paper. "I bought you a ticket to Belfast. From there, you have a flight booked to Newcastle. A rented car is already booked that will take you to Heathrow, where there is a standby reservation on the first flight to Vienna. Once in Vienna, go to this address. I paid for the first month under the name 'Flynn Connel'. Stay there until this mess is cleared out. Here is some money, too. But I am afraid you'll have to find some work to do once you're over there. The flat has a landline. Do not call me; I will call you when it's safe." Shane was speechless. He had questions for his sister. Foremost, he wondered where she found the money to organise everything. But before he could say anything, she threw his backpack on the bed. "Hurry up," she ordered him, "we don't have much time, and you need to get to that plane to Vienna before they realise you're gone. I'll wait for you outside."

18

Libbie was looking at her distorted reflection in the cracked glass. The flower vase was not supposed to hit the mirror, for she had aimed at Michael but had missed him completely. He thought he could get rid of her by putting an end to their story.This was not the first time he'd tried to do so, and she'd always managed to change his mind, but this time was different. The coldness in Michael's eyes alarmed her.He really wanted to end their story and was prepared to tell his wife everything, and to Paul, if necessary. Libbie didn't mind telling Bernadette herself, if it meant walking out of their respective marriages and finally being together, but she knew Michael would have begged his wife for forgiveness and ruined everything.

"How pathetic!" murmured Libbie, pouring herself another drink. She still remembered the first time she saw her lover at the petrol station. She knew well who Michael was. She had come to Seacross, Dublin from London, full of expectations for her life with her new husband, Paul. Her first husband, Jeff, was twenty years older than she, he was an overweight, charmless man but he was rich and generous. For five years, he treated her like a queen. Unfortunately, her kingdom crashed the day the police arrived at their doorstep. Jeff, along with a couple of politicians and some Russian businessmen, had been the object of an investigation lasting for over a year, and when the police eventually had enough evidence of their illegal activities, they arrested him for money laundering and financial fraud. The police searched everything—the house, the office, the boat. They froze the bank accounts and confiscated all assets. It took months for Libbie to clear her name with Interpol, until they eventually believed she had nothing to do with her husband's business. One long year of legal battles left Jeff with a conviction and Libbie with nothing but huge legal fees and bills to pay. She took on whatever job she could find, but whatever she earned was never enough. One night, she met a handsome Irish man, who was charming in his own shy way. He was sweet, and he had a big bulk of cash to spend at the bar where she worked as a pole dancer. Since that night, he became a regular, a couple of times a month, he stopped by and left generous tips for her. One night, he waited for her to finish her show at the bar and offered to buy her a drink. After a few weeks, he waited for her again, only this time, it was her turn to buy him a pint.

"Let's make a toast to my divorce," she cheered. The divorce papers came in with the post that same morning. Libbie and Jeff were no longer husband and wife, and from then on, his legal bills were no longer her concern or problem anymore. The nightclub where Libbie worked had just one unbreakable rule for its dancers: the girls could not hang out with customers. It wasn't due to her boss's concern for the girls' safety, but more to his fear of losing good business if his best customers saw them outside the workplace. The girls were free to fool around with whomever they wanted, on the condition that the lucky men kept spending their money inside the club. That was, after all, the only reason there were private rooms on the second floor. That night, Libbie had to cover for a sick colleague, and she was supposed to return to the stage for a second show. "Fuck the show. My hotel is not far," Paul said. Though the music was loud, the barman, with his good hearing, heard him and pushed the button under the counter to call for security. One of the bouncers appeared within seconds. He was a huge guy whose tie looked like it could tear at any moment because of the pressure in his oversized neck. "Is everything ok here?" he asked Libbie. Before she could reply, he turned to Paul and ordered, "Finish your drink and move, man. We don't like customers who bother the girls."

Paul got up from his seat with the clear intention of protesting but Libbie was quick to get between the two men, "It's ok, Marvin. He was doing nothing wrong. I will be up on the stage in a minute." Libbie had already seen what Marvin was capable of, and there was no way Paul stood a chance against him. Paul, on the other hand, seemed unintimidated by Marvin's size.

"I've got this. Don't worry, love," he said to Libbie with his strong Irish accent before moving her aside gently. Paul took a step forward to get closer to the other man.

"Don't you think I don't know the rules? The problem is I'm not a regular customer here. I am about to be this lady's fiancé. And I will be so gracious to let her perform the second show, before bringing her somewhere more romantic and maybe even proposing to her. And as for you, you big fat neck monkey, you can fuck off and go back to your cage."

For a few seconds, there was complete silence until Libbie was called back to the stage. Paul asked for another drink, and leaning with his back on the bar, he waited for the show to start. Marvin disappeared toward the same direction he had arrived. After Libbie finished her show, she went straight to the backstage to remove the heavy makeup caked on her face. She slipped back into her normal clothes, and once back in the club, she was pleasantly surprised to see that Paul was still there.

"You are still here?"

"Of course, I am. What kind of prick would let his fiancée walk home alone at this time of night? Shall we?" said Paul, as he offered Libbie his arm and they went out together.

"You know, it is an excellent thing that you had obtained your divorce. Otherwise, I would have had to wait to marry you, and I am not good at waiting." Paul's words made Libbie break into a loud laugh. She thought he was joking, but he was not. Two weeks later, were married.

After Libbie moved to Ireland, it was immediately clear that Paul was not what she thought he was. She knew his money was not honest money, but she never imagined he was a mule for a drug-dealing ring either. She figured him to be a big deal in the organisation; yet, he was nothing but a cleaned up low-life junky instead. In the beginning, it was not too bad: good money kept cashing in, and they had that gorgeous beautifully renovated big house that he inherited from his parents until he screwed everything up. The house, the money, and everything had gone. Once again, Libbie had lost everything. She hated her husband, and she hated that shithole of a village where he brought her to live. In this deep desolation, her encounter with Michael was a sign of fate. He was the knight in shining armour, who arrived to rescue her. Everything was going for the best until her charming prince started to talk about ending their story. *Nonsense*, though Libbie, *he was just confused*. She only had to clear his mind, and if her husband and his wife were the problem, then she would take care of them.

19

Sergeant McCabe was a real middle-aged Garda officer cliché: bald, overweight, and always with a cup of coffee to go in his hand. If he were the character in an American movie, he would have accompanied his coffee with doughnuts, but because his wife was desperately and unsuccessfully trying to keep his cholesterol and weight under control, he was only allowed homemade scones baked without sugar. He was a Seacross boy, born and bred in the village. His father was a Gardaí too. More specifically, his father was the Gardaí who arrested Shane Flynn that night, many years ago. Sgt McCabe knew Shane since they were kids, even if they never really hung out together. Shane went to a private school, while he went to the local community college, along with most of the village's kids. He remembered the speculation around the reasons Shane had gone to boarding school. He had never been the most sociable guy or the most straightforward, but he had never been trouble either. However, he didn't comply with what the villagers believed to be the norm. Nowadays, someone like Shane would be considered "normal" but back in those days, wearing long hair, and not attending church, and even worse, not being involved in the local GAA club, only meant you were a "weirdo". Then, there was the fact that he was friends with Paul Mulligan, and everybody knew Paul was potential trouble, just like his brother and father before him. Sgt Billy McCabe liked Shane Flynn, merely because Shane Flynn liked him and made his primary school days easier and less lonely. He was chubby and nerdy, but Shane didn't care. He talked and played with him in the yard and sometimes even shared his lunch with him. Billy's mum never packed enough in his lunch box, and to this day, that didn't change except that now, his wife packed his light lunches and not his mother. Billy's and Shane's quasi-friendship brusquely ended with secondary school, when they took separate ways. Despite feeling disappointed that Shane was going to St. Joseph's Brothers boarding school for the boys, Billy had not found it so strange or obscure. The Flynn family had plenty of money, and his sister, Clarisse, attended boarding school as well.

When they arrested Shane, Billy's father woke him up in the middle of the night to ask him about the Flynn boy. Billy had nothing to say to him because, after sixth grade, he never had anything to do with him again. Even after secondary school, they had no interaction as Shane went to college in the States and even once he came back, they hung out in different social circles. Despite the distance that had grown between them, Billy didn't believe Shane would have done such a thing, or to be more precise, "Allegedly done" as he kept reminding his father. Unfortunately, Sgt McCabe Sr.'s mind was already set. "Oh, come on, don't be so naïve, son. Everybody knows the boy has always been strange." In that moment, and for the first time, Billy McCabe questioned his father's impartiality.

If being an introvert and wearing long hair meant guilt, then maybe Shane was guilty of that, but in all the years he had known him—even if superficially—he never had any reason to think wrongly of him. Shane's case reminded Paul of those American kids who were convicted of the sexual assault and murder of a young boy, and who was then ultimately acquitted. The accused were convicted based on the way they looked and their ideas, rather than the evidence presented against them. Dark clothes, dark makeup and a passion for the occult. He knew the comparison was a bit extreme, but he felt somehow his father's judgement was compromised by his mentality and the village's gossips. Since he was a little boy, Billy McCabe wanted to serve justice. Not because he wanted to follow in his father's footsteps, but because he wanted to have a role in society. Billy loved the idea of being a guardian for the ones who needed protection. In addition, he believed that being a policeman would also give him authority and respect. People might still not hold him in the highest regard, but they had to respect him and obey him. To the immense disappointment of his parents, who wanted him to go to university and study law, Billy McCabe Jr. joined the Garda Siochana College instead. He didn't want to study law; he wanted to be the law. Sgt McCabe Sr.'s hostile position toward his son's choice of a career ended when he saw how happy his son was. He and his wife had always been proud of their boy. In the end, all they wanted was for him to be happy and to be doing what he liked, even if it meant risking his life for a ridiculous salary. During the three years Billy spent training at the Garda Siochana College, father and son became close and turned to each other for advice. Billy felt to do real police work every time his father involved him in his cases and in particular, the most exciting and complicated that, in total honesty, was a rarity in the dormant Seacross, until the day the whole town woke up to a tragedy. The robbery and murder at the convenience store shook and changed the village irremissibly. Billy studied the case with his father, but his conclusions were different from those of his father. He believed in Shane's innocence, and his little investigation proved him right. Billy never knew if Shane was aware of his role in the investigation, but he didn't care. All he cared about was bringing about justice. However, Paul Mulligan was well aware of Billy McCabe Junior's involvement, and never stopped blaming him for his misfortune. Paul never missed the chance to showcase his dislike for the young local officer publicly, and when Billy became a sergeant and later took over his father's role, their rivalry increased. The new chief of the local Garda Siochana wouldn't let Paul get away with anything, to which Paul would reciprocate by giving Billy the middle finger every time he saw him. Over the years, Paul had become a regular overnight guest at the station for erratic driving, antisocial behaviour, and other petty crimes, on top of his primary convictions as a drug dealer.

20

"Seacross Garda Siochana," Annette, the young Gardaí in charge of the reception and everything her boss told her to do or didn't want to do himself, answered the phone. She turned white as a ghost as the voice on the other end of the line reported the shooting of a man. At first, Annette doubted what she heard, but when the voice on the phone repeated what happened and gave the address of the crime scene, she knew it was real. The anonymous caller didn't give her time to ask any questions before hanging up the phone. The sergeant was out running a few errands, as the station was not exactly the busiest in the country. There was a time when it was proposed to keep the station open only in the mornings, but the villagers strongly opposed the idea. Apparently, having a Garda station open full-time was a fount of extreme reassurance for the town. Consequently, the station was kept open and operative, but only as a substation of the nearest town, Barrystown. As a substation, only two guards were assigned: a simple rank Gardaí and a sergeant as the chief officer. Due to the low rate of crime in Seacross, the chief and his deputy could easily afford to take some time off to take care of their personal business, especially during the weekdays, since on weekends, they were sometimes asked to aid in Barrystown.

Sgt McCabe had just returned to the car after paying for petrol when he heard a panicking Annette calling him on the radio. She had not reported the phone call straight away, in case it was a prank and would have made her look like a fool. However, the fear that it might have been true took over, and Annette realised it could have been even worse to be blamed of incompetence. Billy had to ask her twice to repeat what she was saying, as she was too agitated and he couldn't understand what she was saying.

"Ok, Annette, calm down, relax. I am going to have a look. Let's hope it's a sick joke."

"Yes, sir, as you say, boss. But, if it is a prank, you won't get upset with me?"

"No, Annette, I would be upset if it was true and you didn't tell me about it. Then, we would both look like idiots. Now, I'll go and will let you know."

Annette eventually relaxed; she'd done the right thing. Up to a couple of years ago, Billy McCabe would have been excited about a possible murder in his town and normally still was. Just right now, with his cholesterol issues and low energy level due to the raw low protein diet he was following, he felt it was not the right time to engage in a big case. He had to admit, the idea of solving a murder case was appealing, but he wondered if he was up to. He would find out soon. Given the conditions of the road up to Green Hills, he was thankful that the government had provided him with an SUV patrol car. However, his belly still wobbled due to the potholes in the road, and he hated it. He pulled over opposite Shane Flynn's house gate and took the path through the woods down to the field. By the time he reached the open field, he was out of breath. He stopped to regain some energy and looked around trying to remember which way the secret passage went to access the property. He was sure there was one, as he remembered using it as a child a couple of times to go play with Shane. After two failed attempts, he finally took the right path through the woods. As an officer of the law, he knew that what he was doing was technically considered trespassing, but before making it official and asking Shane Flynn to access the land, he wanted to see if the report was true. As soon he approached the field, which was part of Shane's back garden, Sgt McCabe could see something laying on the ground. As he got closer, he could see it was the body of a man. He had been shot twice in the chest. There was no pulse.

"Annette, call Phoenix Park and alert the Technical Bureau, then close the station and come here with some yellow tape. I will call Dr Campion to come and make a preliminary assessment of the corpse."

"So, boss, it was true?"

"Yes, Annette. Now, do as I said and do not waste time, nor talk to anyone about it." McCabe hung up the phone and turned to the body. Paul Mulligan would never give him the finger again. His earlier concerns about him being out of shape and too tired for a murder case immediately disappeared. He suddenly became excited at the prospect of having a murder case to solve, on his own. Billy felt nearly ashamed of his earlier thoughts. How could he have become such a lousy and lazy officer? This murder could be the opportunity of a lifetime; the push in his career that he needed. Of course, the identity of the victim and their history made everything more complicated, but Sgt Billy McCabe was confident that nothing could compromise his impartiality. Instinctively, he turned and looked towards the house, from where Shane Flynn was looking back at him from behind the tinted glass of his bedroom window.

21

Both overexcited, the sergeant and his deputy had delimitated the crime scene to avoid any further contamination before the forensic team arrived. "Annette, try Doctor Campion again, she should be here already. Wait for her and call me as soon she arrives. I am going to talk to Mr Flynn. I can't wait any longer. We are on his land after all."

"But it is dark now. Do I have to stay here with the body on my own?"

"Yes, Annette. Paul had a lot of wrong in him, but I doubt he is a zombie who will come alive in the dark."

"Of course, sir. As you say, boss."

Billy loved Annette's devotion to him and didn't deny it made him feel important, but there were times when she really hit his nerves. He switched on the torch he had brought with him, and stood there a moment, unsure whether he should go back through the main road or simply walk down the field to Shane's fenced garden. He could see there was a gate from the backyard to the ground. He decided to try that way first, at least it would spare him the walk all the way back through the woods. Shane greeted Billy like an old friend but did not overdo it on the hospitality. He didn't ask him in and instead, kept him outside for the duration of his visit. He was still in shock from the events of the afternoon and was afraid he would not be able to hide his nervousness for too long. Billy appreciated the fact that Shane didn't pretend to be sorry for Paul's death. In total honesty, he did not think too many would cry over Paul's body. However, he could imagine that many had plenty of motive to wish him dead. As much as Billy didn't want to admit it, Shane was potentially at the top of the list. Unfortunately for him, once again, clues were leading to him. He had a motive and the opportunity. The last thing Sgt Billy McCabe wanted was to go after Shane Flynn. The guy had already had a bad enough experience with the law and besides, the case was still in its early stages. Doctor Campion hadn't even established the murder weapon yet. Nevertheless, he knew that today was only the first of a series of visits he would probably need to pay Shane during this investigation. Annette rang him to say that Dr Campion was there. Billy turned around and could see the two women waving at him with their torches.

"So, Shane, this is pretty much everything I can say right now. You will probably have some mayhem in the field for a couple of days, but hopefully, it won't disturb you too much, and nobody will come further here. I will probably need to talk to you again, but if you can come down to the station first thing tomorrow morning, Annette will take your official statement."

"I don't know what I can say that will be of any use but sure, I will be there."

"Don't worry. It is just routine. We will be asking everybody in the area on their whereabouts and if they saw or heard anything unusual. Are you sure you didn't hear anything? The field is pretty close, and a shot is pretty audible in such a quiet spot."

"No. I told you, I was in my office working and I didn't hear or see anything." If Billy's tone had come out slightly more inquisitive than he intended it to be, then Shane's was definitely overly defensive, and it didn't go unnoticed.

22

"Hey, Doc, we're done with the corpse for the moment."

"Then be as good to bag it for me and send it to the lab." With that, Dr Campion waved goodbye and walked away.

"Bitch!" That was the first and last time Billy and Annette heard Gloria, one of the forensic technicians speak.

"I heard you, Gloria. Nice to hear your voice every once in a while, darling. I will take it as a compliment coming from you."

Nobody talked or moved for a few seconds. After the coroner disappeared into the woods, they all resumed their activities.

"Wow, boss, was that what they call a catfight?" Annette asked.

Billy was quite surprised about the open hostility between the two women. "I suppose so, Annette..."

"Hey, Billy boy. Just to be sure that we fill the forms correctly, will I write the name of your station or your parent station? Seacross is just a substation, right? Is this investigation going to be yours or will some inspector from Barrystown take over?" Tom Philips, the leader of the forensic team said. Philips was the best in his field, but unfortunately, he was also one of the most unpleasant people on Earth.

"Shit," Billy blurted. In all the excitement, he had forgotten to call the district superintendent.

"It's ok, Billy boy; you forgot to ring the big boss, did you? Well, you better do it now and let me know."

Sgt Billy McCabe felt humiliated.

Annette was staring at him, petrified.

"Fuck, boss. I'm sorry. It is my fault; I should have called him or reminded you to do it."

"Don't, Annette, it was not up to you. I should have done it, but with all that happened, I had no time. Certainly, I had not forgotten," Annette nodded, pretending it was true. Billy was grateful for her loyalty.

After half an hour, the inspector from Barrystown arrived at the scene. Billy knew George Polinsky for a long time and thought him to be a good fair and honest man. He never bossed him around, nor interfered. Billy strongly hoped he wouldn't start now. After Billy and forensics gave him a full update, the inspector made a call to the district superintendent.

"They are all a bit nervous lately. Superintendent O'Leary will need to have a word with the district chief superintendent, I suppose. Listen, if he is happy to leave the investigation, I am happy to stay out of your way."

"Thank you, George. I appreciate that." Billy was relieved and turned to Annette to send her home.

"Will I buy you a pint?" Inspector Polinsky offered. The inspector always enjoyed Billy's company. There was something in the clumsy and naïve countryside man that he liked, and he always thought he had a good nose for police work, but not many chances to use it.

23

Seacross might have been a small village, but it sure didn't lack in pubs. The ones on the harbour were the most popular, even during the winter. If the sun was out, people liked having a pint outside, watching the view. Due to his role in the community, Billy was not welcome at certain pubs where the younger customers engaged in drug use. In silent agreement, Sgt McCabe and Investigator Polinsky drove their cars straight to The Snake. The Snake was a little pub beside one of the best steakhouses in the entire county—at least according to Billy. He would often eat at the restaurant, then go for a few at the bar afterwards. The Snake was cosy and had big leather armchairs at every table. Its owner, Dan, was an American who arrived in Ireland 30 years prior in the search for his heritage and never left. Dan's long-term partner was a surgeon, and after Ireland legalised same-sex marriage, they eventually became husband and husband. Normally, the Seacross community would feel quite uneasy with such a thing, but not in Dan and Jerry's case. They had been together since the first day they moved to the village, over fifteen years ago, and everybody respected them. The only gossip ever around them was about the business. According to the informed, the pub was only surviving thanks to Jerry's continuous funding and in fairness, that was no surprise. The pub was no longer ever crowded and hosting the weekly local chess club and women's bridge night didn't guarantee to cover the bills. Billy could clearly remember the days when there was always a queue outside, but then people got fed up with never finding a space and stopped going. However, Billy was still a loyal customer, and so was George Polinsky—when he was in the area.

"Good evening, officers. What an honour to have you both here together," Dan greeted his customers with a big smile. "The usual?" Both men nodded exhaustedly.

"Do you think you can make me a sandwich, too, Dan?" Billy asked, nearly imploring.

"Of course, chief. I might also have some soup left from lunch. Let me see in the kitchen."

"What? I didn't eat any dinner and barely had lunch today," Billy said to George, trying to justify himself and to specify that he was not snacking behind Martha's back. He then realised he had not called her yet. He looked at his watch and his face darkened. She would definitely be worried or furious, or both.

"I need to make a call," he said, standing up to go somewhere more private.

"Say hi to the missus for me," George called after Billy, and in that very same moment, Dan arrived at the table and looked confusedly at George.

"He forgot to call Martha to say he was late," Polinsky said, mocking Billy.

"Oh, boy, I'd better top up his pint with something stronger then, he might need it," Dan replied with sarcasm, and the two men laughed in unison.

In the meantime, in the winter garden, Billy was trying to explain himself to his wife, "Honey, before you say anything, I am so sorry I haven't called you but you are not going to believe what happened today," Billy paused to gauge his wife's reaction.

"Let me guess, you have found a body in Flynn's field."

Billy was surprised. How could she know already? Nevertheless, at least she knew he had a good reason for not calling, "How the hell do you know?" Billy asked impulsively. They had been very careful at the crime scene, so either Shane had said something, but considering the man hardly had a social life it was highly unlikely, or someone leaked it already. But who and to what extent? In a matter of seconds, Sgt McCabe's head filled with thousands of thoughts and worst-case scenarios, including the superintendent, firing him due to his incompetence and not being able to keep things under control. From the other end of the line, Martha could feel Billy's anxiety. She knew her husband, and knew he was most likely hyperventilating, imagining the worst. "Billy, relax, honey. I am the only one to know and only because I rang Annette because you weren't answering your phone. Are you ok, darling? It must have been a shock to see someone you knew dead. I mean, killed. Well, even if it was Paul Mulligan, and I don't mean to be mean." Billy interrupted his wife before she went on for another half hour. When in the mood, Martha could be a real chatterbox.

"Yes, honey, I'm ok. For a moment I thought someone leaked what happened. You know, we're only in the early stages, and I am not even sure I will be in charge of the investigation. George is ok with it, but in the end, it's up to the district superintendent." It was hard for Billy to hide his apprehension from his tone, and Martha didn't fail to notice.

"Of course, you will be, Billy. Now, where are you? Have you eaten something? Will I wait up for you?" Billy was relieved that Martha was not angry with him. The last thing he needed was ending his already-long day with an argument with his wife. He told her not to wait up for him and that he was going to eat something at The Snake with Inspector Polinsky. When he returned, Inspector Polinsky gestured to Dan to bring back the soup he had brought from the kitchen to warm up, as Billy already bit into his sandwich.

"Everything ok with Mrs McCabe?" Dan asked, leaving the soup on the table.

"Absolutely, she was just worried. And now, if you had had enough of my private business, I would like to finish my dinner," the sergeant said, laughing and gesturing at his steaming soup.

"Ah, she is a saint that woman, still wondering how she can stay with a brute like you," Dan joked, while disappearing back behind the bar counter.

"Agreed. To Martha," George said, as he raised his glass to toast.

"To Martha," cheered Billy, raising his glass too and suddenly feeling the desire to go home and hug his wife. Still, after all these years together, her laugh had the power to put him in good mood. Never once in all the years together had Martha ever condemned her husband's work or his devotion to the force. Billy had heard many stories about guards ending up divorced because their wives couldn't cope with their jobs and crazy hours, but Martha was different. Martha had married Sgt Billy McCabe and never regretted it. She never failed to be by his side, whatever it meant.

Billy and Martha had met during a chess tournament. She was nerdy without a doubt, but a damn pretty one. Unfortunately, he had not been the only one to notice her but for once, he had been the quickest to invite her for a drink at the end of the tournament. At the time, Billy McCabe still had most of his hair and a nearly flat stomach. They spent the entire evening chatting and drinking. When they both felt reasonably drunk, they decided to leave the pub. The tournament had been held in Sandymount, in one of Dublin's southern districts, while Billy lived on the north side.

"I hope you won't drive home in this state and on a Saturday night. There will be a lot of checkpoints, and guards can be harsh these days. They would do anything to take the fun away." Martha finished the sentence with a big laugh and a jokingly distorted mocking face. Martha didn't know Billy was a guard and Billy, of course, didn't get offended. On the contrary, he was quite pleased with her remarks, and they gave him the perfect opportunity to impress her. He stopped, took out his badge, and with a pretend-serious tone, replied, "I thought we had reasonable fun tonight." Martha froze on the spot, blushed, covered her mouth with both hands, then started to apologise. Billy managed to keep still and serious for another few seconds before breaking out in a big laugh. Martha looked at him for a moment, then joined him with her sweet and contagious laugh. While they were still laughing uncontrollably, she slid her hand under his arm and they walked away aimlessly. Unfortunately, their obnoxious laughter didn't please the residents of the area, and they soon found out after having a bucket of water dumped on their heads, and a few not-so-kind remarks. Once their initial shock subsided, they burst into laughter once again and ran around the corner to regain their breath.

"I live at the end of that lane," Martha said. You can come in to dry yourself off if you want. I suppose I can trust a guard." Billy couldn't believe his ears and his luck, and secretly blessed and thanked the prick who'd thrown the water at them. He nodded, trying to mask his excitement. Martha had the most beautiful smile he had ever seen. Her wet blond hair was all combed back and her green eyes sparkled in the dark. Her studio apartment was clean and nicely decorated. It smelled of vanilla, exactly like her.

"Take off that wet shirt; I will grab you a towel." Martha disappeared for a few minutes and came back with a towel and a T-shirt. "I'm afraid this is the biggest shirt I have. I'm going to change into something dry too."

Billy watched as she disappeared again to what had to be the bedroom. He dried his hair and torso with the towel and put on the T-shirt Martha gave him. It was a Star Wars T-shirt, probably too big for Martha but definitely too small for him. He looked at his reflection on the sleeping TV screen and felt like an idiot. He removed his trousers as they were also wet. The radiator was running, so he put all his clothes on it, hoping they would dry quickly. Billy had never been in the flat of a girl he had just met—that on its own was enough to make him nervous, not to mention the fact that he was only wearing his underwear and a few sizes too small Star Wars T-shirt. Martha came back wearing a pair of jeans and a white shirt, with the first few buttons left undone. Later, she confessed she had left them undone on purpose.

"Oh, I see you made yourself at home," she said, looking at his bare legs and his boxers.

Billy blushed and started to apologise. "No, it is just that my trousers were wet, too. I didn't mean... you know..."

She looked at him and smiled. "It's Ok. I'll make some tea? Coffee?"

Martha had such a natural way about her that Billy could not help but relax, and after a couple of mugs of coffee, any embarrassment he had felt, disappeared. They chatted until the first light of the morning. The sunrise was magnificent and they both watched it through the window.

"I don't think there is much point in you going home now," Martha said. "I'll get you a blanket. Let's try to sleep for at least a few hours." She went into her bedroom and came out with a blanket.

"Here, you can have the couch. I am sorry, my rule is never to sleep with someone on the first date." She stopped for a minute, then added, "I know we were not on a date, but still, I only met you for the first time tonight." Martha didn't wait for his reply and went to bed. Billy wanted to object and tell her she had actually met him the previous night and that was technically the second day she met him, but he didn't want to push it. He knew she was the one. They saw each other again the following weekend, and both agreed to consider it a second date. And the rest was history.

24

The very same morning, after the finding of Paul's body, Sgt Billy McCabe received a phone call from the district superintendent who confirmed the case was all his. Apparently, neither he or the chief division superintendent had time to bother with the murder of an insignificant low-level criminal. The Garda high ranks were, in fact, busy with a big narcotics operation that so far, had brought the arrest of seventy people between Ireland and Spain.

The statements collected from the residents of Green Hills didn't add anything of particular interest to the investigation. And Annette and Billy decided to focus all their attention on the list of persons who had reasons to harm Paul. The list they filled was quite long, but unfortunately for them, most of the people on it were either already in jail or were after Paul for money, and in that case, had no interest of wanting him dead. So far, the most noteworthy names on Billy McCabe's list of suspects were Shane Flynn and the widow. His gut told him that both trails were a waste of time, but he had to dig further as they were the only leads he had so far.

“Poor woman, do we have to do this now, boss? She has just lost her husband.” Annette didn’t feel comfortable asking Libbie to come to the station and having to interrogate her.

“Remember, Annette, in most cases, it is usually the wife or the husband,” replied Billy, who was also not happy to have to corner the widow in such a moment, yet he couldn’t afford to lose time. Libbie didn‘t play the part of the inconsolable widow, not even for a second; it wouldn’t have looked real anyway, as everybody knew they were separated and knew she’d had enough of him. Billy appreciated her honesty but, at the same time, was impressed with her lack of emotions. At the time of the murder, Libbie stated she was at home on the phone with her internet provider. It was not the best of the alibis but it was easy enough to verify with the phone records.

“So, if that’s all...” Libbie didn’t hide the fact that she considered the meeting a huge inconvenience.

“Yes, that is all, for now. Thank you for your time, Mrs Mulligan, we appreciate it as we know it must be a very distressing time for you.” Billy raised from his chair and escorted Libbie to the door, while an efficient Annette brought over the statement to be signed. Libbie, as though she didn’t want to touch anything inside the office, extracted a gold pen from her purse and signed her statement.

“Jeez, boss, that woman gives me the creeps! You know that old movie with Tom Cruise? The one from your days? My dad used to watch it every time it was on TV. What was it called?” Annette looked up as she thought. “You know what I’m talking about, chief? Tom played a pilot in it.”

"That movie from *my days*, Annette?!" Billy replied. "It's called *Top Gun*, and it's one of the cult movies of the century."

"Yes, *Top Gun*, that's the name," Annette agreed cheerfully as though she had just guessed the right answer on a quiz show.

"Are we going somewhere with this, Annette? Maybe somewhere connected to our investigation?" Billy was more upset about the implication about his age.

Annette blushed, "Yes sir, of course, we are, chief. My point is, you know the other guy, not Tom, the one they called Iceman, yea? The poor widow, here, looks like his female twin." Without giving him time to reply, Annette exited the room. It was now over a year that Annette worked at the station and Billy liked her, but at times, she could come across as weirdly annoying. However, in this case, he could not deny she was right. It would have never crossed his mind to associate Libbie Mulligan to a character from *Top Gun* but Annette was right, she was a cold-blooded woman. Annette went back in Billy's office to bring him a mug of freshly brewed coffee. He was standing at the window still thinking about Libbie Mulligan. Something wasn't adding up, but he couldn't put his finger on it, until Annette reminded him of something.

"Sir, have you noticed that Mrs Mulligan didn't ask when she can have the body back? She couldn't care less about funeral arrangements, etc. Usually, people are adamant to give their loved ones a proper burial. I mean, I understand they were separated, but still..."

That was exactly what Billy couldn't put his finger on. Libbie Mulligan didn't make any inquiries about her late husband –

not about when they would release the body, nor about how he died. In his experience, the relatives were always obsessed with the details. They wanted to know how, when, what and why. But she didn't. She either genuinely didn't care, or she already knew. In either case, it might be worth it to keep an eye on her.

"Annette, get all the information you can about Mrs Mulligan, and see if you can find out if there is some truth behind the gossip of her having an affair with some local."

"Yes, sir, I'm on it, boss."

25

"Hello, Billy. I'm just giving you a courtesy call to say I have finished the autopsy on Mulligan, and that the report will be on your desk by tonight."

"Thank you, Dr Campion. Anything unusual? What about the possible murder weapon?"

"Well, as I had assumed, the cause of death was the second shot. Both shots were fired at close range. The bullet was still inside him, probably a 9 mm, but not of a common issue. Maybe something old fashioned. I am not an expert on that, Billy, I'm sorry. I've sent everything to ballistics. You will need to wait for Philips to get more information about that."

"That's fine, Dr Campion, you've been excellent as usual. Thanks for calling."

"Oh, just one last thing. Judging by the entry and the way the body fell, I say the killer is not particularly tall," she added.

"So, you think it might be a woman, then?"

"Billy, don't put words in my mouth. All I'm saying is that the person you are looking for is likely to be between 5 foot 7 and 5 foot 8. Have a good day."

Billy immediately rang the lab in Phoenix Park.

"Hey, Billy boy, how are you doing?" The more Billy had to deal with Philips, the more he despised him.

"Yes, I have all your results ready, sending you the report now. We found four sets of footprints around the cadaver, excluding yours and your deputy's. One for sure belongs to the victim and the other three most likely belong to two men, size ten and either a woman, size six or a man with pretty tiny feet." Tom Philips could not resist the temptation of laughing at his own joke.

"What can you tell me about the murder weapon?" Sgt McCabe struggled to hide his annoyance.

"Oh, yes, you don't have much of a sense of humour, Billy boy. Let's go straight to business, then. It's been years since I've seen one of these handguns. It is a Ruger semiautomatic. Travellers used to have these crappy things in the nineties. A batch arrived from the UK, they were the cheapest in the commerce. But seriously, man, either your killer likes bad quality vintage, or he had it at the bottom of the wardrobe for a long time. It might be easier than you expect to find a match."

If Dr Campion was right—and she always was—Shane Flynn, on account of his height, couldn't have been the shooter. He was at least 6'2". Then, there were the ballistic results; the murder weapon was a handgun and Shane only owned hunting shotguns. Of course, if Shane had shot Paul, he would not have been that stupid to do it with one of his rifles, but at least Billy could remove him from the top of his list of suspects. Not that he ever actually believed Shane could be a primary suspect but unfortunately, in investigations, clues win over instinct and all the clues seemed to point to him. A few townspeople overheard their argument in the parking lot, only days before Paul was shot dead. Then, there was the crime scene—it was Shane's land. Everything confirmed that Paul went to the crime scene willingly, as his car was found parked on the road. He knew his shooter and was most likely not afraid of him. Maybe this was all a coincidence, or perhaps, it was not and whoever killed Paul, planned it carefully and set Shane up. A part of him wanted to believe this version but his police side had to consider the fact that when he spoke to Shane, he looked nervous, dismissive and was holding something back. But what? He was determined to find out.

26

After he had finished university in Vienna, Shane found a job as a mechanical engineer in a tire factory. One of his main tasks was to test the performance of the tires on the road under different weather conditions. Soon, he began to think about how he could improve the performance of the tires and started to develop what turned out to be an innovative and revolutionary idea. He invented a special paint to help with the adherence of tires on the road. The company showed no interest in investing in him, but Shane firmly believed in his invention. He deposited the patent and continued to look for investors. Thanks to a connection he had made during his studies, he managed to get in touch with a big automotive distributor that agreed to support the cost of the production of his product. By chance, the product landed in the hands of a mechanic for one of the most prestigious Formula One teams. The mechanic immediately recognised the potential of Shane's paint. Within a few years, Shane Flynn's company became one of the most important in Europe, and he managed to accumulate a significant capital in cash and estates.

Before moving back to Ireland, he sold the company but held a few of the stocks in his portfolio to keep the profits coming in. He could comfortably live off what he gained from selling his company, but he invested in a few other things to guarantee constant earning. Soon, it became clear to Shane that sitting and monitoring his investments was not enough. He was bored. Shane Flynn was not ready to retire yet, not full time at least, so he decided to give back the opportunity he had at the start of his career. He started to collaborate with talented young entrepreneurs in need of advice and funds.

That afternoon, he was sitting in his home office, checking the markets and trying to finish the review of a new start-up that had contacted him a few weeks earlier. His loyal Setter Gordon, Polly, was resting at his feet. At her age and because of her hip, that was what she did most of the day. Despite his efforts to concentrate on the papers in front of him, his mind was on Bernadette. She was avoiding him since the finding. He sent her texts and tried to call her but got nothing back, and it was driving him mad. When he moved back, he'd intended to find closure with the past. In the beginning, he thought he would have only found closure from confronting the two people who betrayed him. Paul betrayed his trust and friendship, but Bernadette gave away their love when she refused to believe him and wait for him. When he came back to Seacross, he was angry, resentful and vindictive, but he soon realised he didn't want and didn't need to harm anyone. Paul had already paid enough with his miserable life and Bernadette, well, no matter how much he tried, Shane could never hate her. For years, he thought she had forgotten about him the moment he was gone, but after speaking to her and seeing the light in her eyes when she looked at him, he knew she never did. The afternoon they spent together had bonded them again. The way they kissed, the way they made love: everything indicated that nothing had changed between them. Their feelings were not dead. They were not dead! He still wanted answers and an explanation, but that could wait, and if they never came, he could learn to accept it or at least try. However, he would never be able to learn to live with losing her again. He picked up the phone with the intention to ring her but just when he was about to press the green call button, the gate bell rang. Shane was not expecting anybody. The only visitors he usually had over to see him, they came for business, and today, he had no appointments. Suddenly, his face lit up. It could be Bernadette. She knew as much as he did, that they could not keep ignoring each other. Expectation and excitement rose within him as he opened the gate and ran straight for the front door. His hand was already wrapped around the handle when he gave a last look at himself on the mirror above the console in the hall. He fixed his hair, feeling as ridiculous as a teenager and with a smile on his face, opened the door.

"Sorry to show up like this, Shane, but I need to ask you a few more questions if you don't mind." Billy McCabe removed his cap and dried a drop of sweat running down from his forehead. Shane's smile disappeared and his disappointment was hard to conceal. There were a few seconds of embarrassed silence, then Shane woke up from his limbo.

"Oh, sorry, of course, Billy... I just thought you were someone else. Please, come in." It took a single look for Billy to realise Shane was expecting someone and he couldn't help but wonder who it could be. Shane didn't have friends in the village, but the sergeant clearly remembered that when he came to see him the first time around, he saw two wine glasses on the coffee table through the garden window, and he was pretty sure he spotted lipstick traces on one of them. Maybe Shane just had a secret lady-friend, and this was all he was holding back.

"I am sorry if you're expecting guests, Shane, but it won't take long," Billy apologised, walking through the corridor leading to the living room. Shane nodded and with a gesture of his hand, invited him to take a seat on the couch. The grey Italian leather corner sofa faced the huge windows overlooking a perfectly landscaped backyard that reminded Billy of a Japanese-style garden one saw in the movies. It had probably cost him one year of his salary. It was a pity he couldn't take a picture to show Martha. That would have been highly unprofessional but she would have loved it.

"Oh, all right, Billy, but at this point, I don't really know what I can tell you that would be of any interest for your investigation," Shane answered, feeling nervous and uneasy.

Billy feared this would happen: another witch-hunt had started and he had just put Shane Flynn right at the centre of it. He felt the pain in Shane's words. The past was back to haunt him and now, he was responsible, even if it was the last thing he wanted. Billy wanted to tell his old friend that he believed in him now like he had twenty-three years ago but instead, he sat there in silence.

"I am trying to forget the whole thing, but apparently, you seem determined not to let me do it. Like father, like son, right, Billy?" Shane immediately realised he overreacted. He brusquely got up and went to the window, turning his back to the guard in an attempt to conceal his face, which could give away too much.

"Hey, man, now you are exaggerating. Nobody mistreated you, not now!" Shane turned and Billy gestured for him to sit back down. The two men were now back sitting and facing each other.

"Shane, I am only doing my job here and frankly, I don't think you have anything to do with Paul's murder, simply because I think you are too intelligent to commit such an act and in such circumstances. But unfortunately, you must agree that the man who framed you for murder and ruined your life, was shot dead on your land, and it seems a bit suspicious. I can't afford not to inquire." Billy spoke calmly and Shane seemed to regain his control.

"Sorry, Billy, I overreacted, but you must understand, after what I went through, police still make me nervous. It is not you, but I know the mistakes that you guys can make to close a case."

From Billy's face, Shane knew that he had understood the implications of what he was saying. Sgt Billy McCabe was still the same good and decent human being he remembered from his school days. Shane felt s slight guilt for having lied to him since it was not the police that made him nervous, but the whole situation he got himself involved in. Whether he wanted to or not, he could not tell the truth because in doing so, he would hurt others.

"I know you are only doing your job, Billy... and I will answer all the questions you want, but first, I will get us some coffee. It might clear our minds."

The coffee was only an excuse. What Shane actually wanted was to leave the room, dry his sweaty hands and recompose and prepare himself for the questions he would have to answer. In the kitchen, he opened the tap and splashed his face with some water. Thankfully, he had left the coffee machine switched on. He filled two mugs and went back to the living room. Shane found Billy standing at the French door overlooking the back garden. He could perfectly see the area of the field where they shot Paul, it was much closer to the house than he previously realised, and that made him think. If Shane was home that day, it was highly improbable that he had not heard the gunshots. Of course, the wind could have blown into the opposite direction to deviate the sound, but still, his instinct was saying he had to dig more.

"Thank you," Billy said, taking the mug distractedly, "Do you mind if I look outside? Is the gate to access the field open?" Shane knew Billy was up to something but couldn't attract any more suspicion by being uncooperative.

"I don't know what you are hoping to find but yes, of course, help yourself. The gate chain is only on the inside, just unchain it." Before Billy left to go outside, Shane couldn't resist asking, "I thought you had already collected all the evidence from the crime scene?"

"Oh, yes, forensic is done. I just want to check on something."

While McCabe was out in the backyard, Shane stayed behind and waited in the house. Billy walked through the garden and out into the field, when a noise captured his attention. At first, he couldn't identify it, then it was clear it was a dog barking; it was not close, but if it was within earshot. it should have been visible as well. He looked around. It was not coming from the woods, so it had to come from the house. From behind a window on the second floor of the house, there was a dog barking. He could only see a vague shape behind the tinted glass but that was enough. Sgt McCabe saw and heard what he came for. When Billy was back at the house, Shane was waiting for him at the garden door. A big black and brown dog was by his side, presumably the one he saw upstairs from the field. When Billy started walking into the garden, the dog began to growl but immediately stopped when Shane pat her head. Slightly intimidated, Billy kept walking.

"I didn't know you had a dog."

"Oh, yes, this is Polly. She has been with me for many years now. She is an old lady and had her hip recently operated, so I am trying to keep her resting. Her hearing is not the best anymore but when she realises there is someone around, her guarding instinct comes back."

Billy followed Shane back into the house and straight to the hall towards the front door—a clear signal that his visit was over, at least where Shane was concerned.

"Thank you for your time, Shane, but I might have to come back with Annette for some tests if you don't mind."

"I don't think I have any other choice, do I?" Shane sharply replied, then tried to laugh to deviate the attention from his answer. Billy didn't reply but put his cap back on and opened the door of his car.

27

Bernadette was having coffee upstairs at Maude's cafe, thinking about why she was there. If she was trying to avoid Shane, it was the worst place to be. Over the months after Shane moved back, Maude's cafe had become the place where she'd not only go to enjoy her own company but his as well. Bernadette knew Shane was back but never ran into him until the day they found themselves queuing up together to order. It was the first time they had seen each other and talked in twenty-three years. The initial awkwardness was hard to break, but in the end, they sat together and chatted for over two hours. After that, Bernadette and Shane started to accidentally but regularly meet at the cafe. Shane later found the courage to confess that it was not a coincidence that they had run into each other the first time. He had followed her because he wanted to see her and talk to her. Gradually, the feelings from the past resurfaced, and their bond started coming back. Bernadette knew she was going through a dangerous path, but she couldn't stop. She never mentioned anything to Michael about seeing Shane. Their chats were innocent, yet she felt she had to keep them secret. Another secret to keep. It looked like she was holding a secret from every man in her life. She was lying to all three of them.

Bernadette was absorbed in her thoughts, and when the church bells rang, they nearly gave her a fright. From her table, she could see the entrance of the church on the other side of the road. When the massive oak double front door opened and revealed the altar with the big cross behind it, Bernadette thought back to the last time she was in a church: it was for her father's funeral. Despite her name, Bernadette had never been a religious person. There was a time when she hated her pompous Catholic name. She was raised Catholic and came from two fervent religious parents, who failed on passing their faith over to her. Michael, on the other hand, had been born and raised Protestant, but precisely like his future wife, he never cultivated his faith. They married with a small ceremony in the register office, and when Samuel came along, they decided to raise him under no faith. After moving to Seacross, where minds were not as open as in Dublin, Bernadette feared he could feel like an outcast—something that thankfully never happened in the end. People still held onto traditions and too often went over the top with first communion parties and weddings that always resembled the royal ones, but they were not queuing to go to church on Sunday morning. She watched the small crowd climbing the church's steps for the last farewell to Paul Mulligan. They were not mourners; they were gossipers and they were curious. There were some bigots, too. Paul's funeral was the event of the day. His violent death gave unexpected notoriety to a little sleeping village. Bernadette could imagine some of the villagers searching the newspapers for the articles about the murder. Their search for those statements given under the pretence of a false reluctance to the journalists arrived from all over Ireland. An involuntary smile naturally formed on Bernadette's lips as she thought of all the young and old carefully cutting articles to keep as a memory of their fifteen minutes of fame. On some nights, she still had nightmares about the killing, and the possible discovery of her presence at the scene. Gradually, that overwhelming sense of guilt she initially felt had started to fade away, leaving more space for the memory of the pleasure that afternoon gave her. The last little group of "mourners" gathered in and the show was over. Bernadette was ready to leave when she saw one last person climb the church steps: it was Shane. He didn't enter; he stayed by the door the whole time. She instinctively sat back, pretending to have some drink left in the big mug that she was now nervously moving in little circles on the table. The young waiter, who was already on her way to clean up after her, retroceded when she saw her customer sitting back. Bernadette stared at the church's gate, and for a moment, she didn't know if she hoped or feared that Shane would turn and look up at her.

"And even if he does, then what?" she murmured to herself. "With the way you're treating him, do you really think he'll still bother with you?" These kind of conversations with herself had become a habit. Maybe it was because she could only confide in herself. Bernadette desperately missed being able to talk to Jane but was not prepared to disappoint and hurt her best friend. The truth was, she had lied to everybody who cared about her for 23 years, and she kept lying.

The mass was over, and Bernadette had lost sight of Shane in the crowd exiting the church. The black van of the funeral director followed by the widow's limousine lead a small motorcade to the graveyard for the burial. Bernadette didn't know why but she followed the procession. The Catholic cemetery was just outside the village. As the church was on the main street, there was no space around for any burial site. The cemetery was much bigger than Bernadette remembered, and it was evident that over the years they'd made many interventions to create more space. Bernadette had no reason to go to that cemetery at all as both her parents expressed the desire to be cremated. She parked as far away as possible from the other cars. She observed the burial from a distance. There was no speech from anyone, and after the priest gave his blessing and the casket was let down into the grave, people started to leave. Some just went straight to their cars, while others stopped to give one last handshake to the widow to reinstate their condolences. On her way back to the car, Bernadette passed Libbie and noticed she had caught her eye. Maybe it was her guilt that was making her see things, but she had the feeling Libbie checked her out. But why? They didn't even know each other. Bernadette gave her a nod and lowering her eyes, she kept walking.

"She was probably curious to know what I was doing hiding back there," Bernadette reassured herself. However, the little voice in her head didn't agree. "Was she? Just as simple as that?"

"Of course, she was. What other business could the poor widow have with me?" Bernadette promptly replied to herself.

"Come on, Bernie. You came here not because you are a curious bigot like most of the other villagers, but because you were hoping to meet *him*, to see *him* and now that you haven't, you don't know if you are relieved or disappointed." That voice had no intention to leave her alone but it was right, and Bernadette found herself blushing at the thought of

Shane, of their afternoon together, of his hands running over her body. She kept walking with her head down but the gravel on the path made it impossible not to be aware that someone was walking behind her. Bernadette smelt that unique Creed aftershave belonging to her previous life and immediately knew who it was. This time, she didn't accelerate her pace to lose him. Instead, she slowed down and let him get closer until she reached her car and turned around to face him.

"We need to talk, Bernie. You can't keep avoiding me." Shane's voice was determined but gentle.

"I know, Shane." She wanted to tell him that she was sorry and wanted to confess all her desire for him.

Bernadette tried to tell him the truth, the whole truth, but she was frozen. Shane stepped closer to her and she moved back against her car. The car door handle pushed into her lower back, but she felt no pain. Her hand spontaneously touched his, and a shiver ran through them both. They could equally feel it. They had no time to speak before more steps on the gravel disturbed their moment. They were not alone; someone else was still there. Bernadette looked straight behind Shane's back and suddenly turned blank in fear. Shane instinctively turned his head and understood what caused her pallor. Bernadette rushed to untangle her hands from Shane's and by the time he turned toward her, she had already opened the door to get into the car. She looked at him from inside the vehicle and without saying a word, smiled at him. Shane smiled back, and she saw in his eyes that he now knew he still had a place in her heart. Shane patted the roof of Bernadette's car; he could let her go for now. Everything else could wait because he no longer had any more doubts: she was still his.

Sgt Billy McCabe's steps were resonating heavy on the graveyard's path. His notebook in his hands still didn't hold any notes. The funeral revealed no surprises and no new faces that could raise any suspects or leads. This investigation was going nowhere, but he was sure there was something he was missing. He knew it was right in front of him; he just had to figure it out and connect the dots. Maybe he had to listen to his wife and start doing those sudoku quizzes she loved so much. They apparently make the mind more flexible. To his surprise, he saw there was still someone there, aside from him. Pleased to see he had found a way to bury the past, Sgt McCabe waved at Shane and Bernadette from a distance. If he only knew!

28

"I thought you were going to be there today." Libbie's tone was a mix of anger and sadness.

"Doing what? Don't be ridiculous." Michael's incapacity to disguise his annoyance surprised them both, and they both fell silent. Libbie could be dangerous, and now that Paul had died and she had nothing to lose, she was even more so. Michael had learned not to cross her. "Listen, honey, I am sorry. I didn't want to snap at you, but it has been a long and busy day." At the other end of the line, his mistress was not talking and Michael could only hear her heavy breath broken by false sobs, that only increased his annoyance, but he had to play along.

"I know, and I am sorry, it is just that I thought...Well, never mind." Libbie eventually broke her silence. "...I just would have liked to have someone there at my side. You should have seen all the villagers looking at me—the wife of the murdered junky. I bet they were there just out of curiosity. Gosh, I hate this shit hole of a town." She recited the parts of the victim and the neglected woman in love with perfection, but Michael was not falling for it anymore. While she was still ranting on the phone about how the villagers were gossiping about her and the fact that she was not even living with Paul anymore, he was only worried about the rumours that went around about her having a married boyfriend who was paying for her apartment. As long as they were cautious, it was going to be ok. The problem, however, was that she was getting impatient and less careful to a point that sometimes, he had the impression she was sloppy on purpose, and that she wanted them to get caught. He had to end this affair but now it was not that easy, and Michael regretted having started it in the first place.

"Fuck, fuck, fuck," he screamed, slapping his fist on the top of a cupboard containing his instruments, incapable of controlling his nerves. He lived in fear of what Libbie could say or do to ruin his marriage and felt he was always watching over his shoulder.

"Darling? Are you still there?" He took off the mute from the phone and ended the conversation with the promise to go and visit her later.

Michael punching the cupboard did not go unnoticed. "Doctor Greaney, is everything all right?" the nurse asked, knocking on the door to check on him.

"Yes, sorry, Sally, I just dropped something. Everything is fine." Michael recomposed himself and opened the door to show her everything was perfectly fine. "You can send in Mrs Queen, thank you. She is the last patient, is she?"

"Yes, Doctor Greaney."

"Ok then, lock the entrance and come in to help."

The receptionist was off for three weeks on honeymoon, and so in the meantime, he and Sally were covering for her. In normal circumstances, Michael would have asked Bernadette to cover for Camille, the receptionist, but not with Libbie around and out of control as she was.

"Hi, I was dying to see you." Libbie threw her arms around Michael's neck. She was wearing a black silk gown, slightly open at the front, which exposed her braless breasts. She kissed him and moved his hands on her hips and back on her lower back. Using all his self-control, Michael stepped back from her tempting body.

"No. Not tonight, Libbie. I can't stay. I just stopped by to see how you were and if you needed something."

Libbie went to the kitchen and poured herself a glass of wine. Michael knew she was upset.

"How I feel, Michael? How do you think I feel? I feel like shit, and I feel lonely." She took a sip of wine and went on, "And just when I needed you the most, you disappeared. You neglected me."

"Come on, Libbie. Wait a minute... you know that is not true."

"Right now, Michael, the only thing I know is that you are treating me like shit. You make me beg for your time. What am I for you, Michael? Am I just a fuck? But a damn good one! Isn't it?" She stepped closer to him, and after untying her gown, she let it slip to her feet, revealing her perfect body. Michael picked it up and handed it back to her.

"Don't embarrass yourself."

Libbie grabbed the gown back from Michael, and after covering herself, she sat down, letting some tears descend over her face.

"Don't you see what you do to me? Do you think I like to humiliate myself like that?" A part of Michael felt sorry for her but the other didn't trust her. He took a chair and sat in front of her, wiped the tears away from that beautiful face and hugged her. She had won again. He succumbed to her power, and they made love.

'Stupid fucking idiot.' Michael despised the weak man he had become. In the living room, Libbie was cooking and without turning as though they were a normal married couple, she asked if he preferred spaghetti or pasta.

"I told you I couldn't stay. I am late already. I didn't say anything to Bernadette about being late or staying for dinner. I have to go home."

"So that's it? You got what you wanted and now you go home?" Libbie's tone was calm but full of a lucid rage, and so without saying a word, Michael took his phone out from his jacket pocket and rang his wife to say he was going to be late. He then unscrewed a fresh bottle of white wine and poured two glasses. Libbie lifted hers and invited Michael to toast. "How nice it would be to do this every day," she said. Michael knew the response she was expecting but could not speak it without betraying his real feelings.

"You know, darling, your wife was at the funeral, but I have been a good girl and didn't say anything to her... even if I could have." Michael froze and a shiver ran down his spine. What in hell was Bernadette doing at the funeral and why didn't she say anything to him?

29

"Annette, get out all the witnesses' statements for the Mulligan case and come to my office," Sgt McCabe shouted, entering the station. Anette checked her watch; it was going to be another late night without being paid for her overtime, but she didn't care. They were working at a homicide. God only knew if she would have had that chance again.

"Here boss," she dropped the folder on the desk and took a seat opposite Billy. It didn't take long to find what they were looking for and after agreeing on what to do next, they called it a night.

"Good morning, Shane. I am sorry to bother you again, but I need to enter your property and check on something from your house. I was wondering if Annette and I can come over in the afternoon?" Shane's hesitation and tone were suggesting he was not happy about the whole thing, but he couldn't refuse without looking suspicious. Billy stopped the car outside Shane's gate, and Annette rang the bell. Shane was standing at the door, with an unwelcoming expression. Billy extended his hand to shake Shane's. "Thank you, Shane, for allowing us to do this. I appreciate your collaboration. I promise it won't take long."

Annette nodded and followed her boss out onto the field like a loyal puppy.

"Annette, just stand here and look at the house. Can you see anything?"

"No boss, the windows are those expensive ones—the ones where you can't see inside during the day."

"Exactly, Annette, but from the inside, you can see outside. Now, I want you to go back to the house and ask Mr Flynn if you can access his bedroom. I am going to try something."

Annette went back inside and asked Shane to escort her to his bedroom. Shane didn't ask any questions since he now began to understand what McCabe was after.

"I will be downstairs if you need me," he coldly said to Annette before leaving the room.

Annette went to the window from where she had a clear vision of her boss and the entire field. The house was marvellous, and the view could take one's breath away. For a moment, she forgot why she was there and just imagined what it would be like to wake up every morning with such a view. If she lived in a house like this, she would make sure to always dress appropriately for her status. She would wear silk blouses and tailor-cut trousers every day. Annette didn't like skirts. Two blank shots woke her up from her daydream. Annette's cheeks blushed uncontrollably in shame for letting those frivolous thoughts distract her from duty. The sergeant joined his deputy upstairs, "Thanks, Annette, we can go now."

"But sir, what...? " Annette was puzzled but didn't have time to finish her sentence.

"I'll tell you in the car. Now, let's go."

Shane and Polly were waiting for them at the bottom of the stairs. Polly was agitated and growled at the two officers as they passed.

"I am sorry, she is not dangerous, just an old cranky lady and the shots upset her," As soon the words left his mouth, Shane regretted them.

"Thank you very much for your help and availability, Shane. I will keep in touch if there is any development." Shane nodded and closed the door behind him as fast as he could.

"So, boss, you want to tell me what is going on?" Annette didn't even wait to be out of the driveway.

"I think you know, Annette. Did you hear the shots from the bedroom?"

"Yes, sir, loud and clear, as much as I heard the bloody dog barking after them."

"And you could see me?"

"Perfectly, boss."

"That is my point, Annette. If he was home the day of the murder, he must have heard the shots and most likely saw someone in the field. The other day, when I was here on my own, I could hear his dog barking from out there, with all the windows closed."

"But, boss, he could have been in the shower or in bed."

"In the middle of the day? Come on, Annette."

"Ok, let's say people shower only and religiously in the morning. What if he was in his office working? It's at the back of the house."

Billy hated Annette's sarcasm.

"But he never mentioned it. If it was me, that would have been the first thing to say, to get myself out of trouble, right?"

"Assuming that you have a guilty conscience, yes!"

Billy could see Annette's point but he also knew how nervous Shane was around the police.

"Maybe," Billy continued. "but there is also the fact that he said he was alone when I saw two glasses on the table and one had lipstick on it."

"Sorry to not agree with you, boss, but you said it yourself, maybe there is just a lady friend he doesn't want people to know about."

Annette was probably right, but still, things didn't add up.

"And speaking of lady-friend, sir, look what I found on the carpet in the bedroom." Annette took a gold sequin out of her pocket, "If Mr Flynn does have a secret lady-friend, she must dress fancy."

"Stop the car, Annette. You go back to the station. I need to go back and have another word with Mr Flynn. I will walk down to the village when I am done. Some exercise won't hurt, and Martha will be happy."

Perfectly aware that Shane wouldn't be welcoming, Billy McCabe rang the bell at the gate, for the second time in a few hours.

"Billy, either you start to fancy me or to despise me." Shane didn't exactly welcome Billy back inside the house, but he politely invited him into the kitchen and poured them both a cup of coffee.

"Now, Shane. I know how difficult this can be for you and believe me, I am the first one who doesn't want to cause you any more trouble than necessary."

"Maybe you should try harder, Billy."

"Maybe you should start telling the truth, Shane. I know you are holding something from me."

The colour completely vanished from Shane's face and before he could speak, the sergeant went on, "Annette and I just proved you must have heard the shots from the house, unless you were in the shower or working in your office, but you hadn't mentioned any of this when you were first questioned." Billy added, anticipating what Shane could have objected. "It is simply a matter of the fact that you have been quite vague about your whereabouts of that afternoon, whether inside or outside the house. Now, put yourself in my shoes. What should I think?" The question was left hanging in the air.

"Oh, come on, Billy, I haven't killed the man, and you know it. You know me! Maybe I was in the shower, or maybe I was in the study doing something. I don't fucking remember what I was doing when the poor bastard was killed, ok?" Shane's white face turned red, and he brusquely got up from his chair. He was nervous and scared of betraying himself and Bernie with his words. For a second, he thought of the possibility to come clean and tell him everything, but how could he do that to Bernadette? The lie went too far, and Paul had screwed him over once again without even knowing it.

“Listen, I have nothing to do with this bloody murder. Am I sorry the bastard is dead? No, I’m not, but I swear to God, I didn’t kill him. I didn’t move back for revenge. I am trying to live my life without crossing paths with anybody and even less with my past.”

“Well, you seem to be back and quite friendly with Bernadette!” Billy thought of this when he saw them after the funeral and when he saw them at Maude’s cafe together. People always tended to ignore him, but he saw more than the villagers thought.

“You leave Bernadette out of this; do I make myself clear?” Shane was livid and his fists were tight. “And now, I think it is better you leave, and if you come close to Bernie or me again, I will sue you for harassment.”

Billy didn’t expect such a strong reaction; it was a miracle Shane didn’t punch him in the nose. He had definitely pushed the wrong button or the right one, depending on which side one looked at it, and he was pleased with himself. Halfway through Green hills, Sgt McCabe had already regretted having sent Annette away with the car, but his visit to Shane’s was worth the effort. The picture was becoming clearer.

30

That night, when he came home after seeing Libbie, Michael confronted Bernadette about her presence at the funeral. At first, she tried to stay vague, but when she realised he already knew, she had to tell him everything. Michael had gone way too far with his reaction, but it was the only way to discover if his wife suspected something about his affair. At the end of their quarrel, there were no doubts that Bernadette went to the funeral only out of curiosity and that she suspected nothing.

The following morning, Bernadette was still upset about the argument she had the previous night with her husband. Michael had come home late from work and questioned her about what she had done and where she had gone during the day. At first, she had not mentioned Paul's funeral; she didn't want to say anything about her encounter with Shane as she was too afraid to betray herself with her words. When Bernadette realised Michael already knew she went to the funeral, it was too late. He was furious and accused her of lying; Michael accused her of never having buried the past and of being insensitive and disrespectful towards him. Bernadette could understand he was hurt, she lied to him, but it was not the end of the world. As much as he was concerned, she lied only about her whereabouts of the day, nothing malicious. Where was all that rage and resentment coming from? She had never seen him like that and wondered if whoever had told him they saw her at the funeral, told him she was with Shane too. That was the only explanation for such a violent reaction, but as their discussion went on, it became apparent that Michael was oblivious to whatever was going on between his wife and her former lover. The atmosphere at the breakfast table was tense, and they both looked at each other in search of suspicious signs. Michael drained his mug of coffee, got up and apologised for his behaviour from the previous night. Bernadette gently patted his hand that was resting on her shoulder. The crisis was over.

After Michael left to get dressed, Bernadette could eventually check her phone that kept vibrating inside her cardigan pocket. It was Shane. The time she dreaded to see his name on the phone display was gone. Now, she hoped for it, and every time it happened, her stomach was invaded by a swarm of butterflies. Shane knew not to ring her in case Michael was around. The text was brief: he wanted to see her and texted her the code to the gate. She waited for Michael to leave and went straight upstairs, followed by Pedro and Berta. The dogs jumped on Bernadette's bed with their daily walk in mind, prepared to wait for their owner to get ready and go. Bernadette threw a look at her dogs and felt sorry for them. "Sorry, guys, no walk this morning." Berta and Pedro seemed to understand they were not going anywhere when their owner didn't just slip into her tracksuit but instead, opened the drawer of the good underwear and then carefully picked out her outfit.

Shane knew it was careless having Bernadette walk over to his house, but those accidental encounters at Maude's could not go on anymore either. Sooner or later, someone would have noticed them and rumours would begin to spread. He didn't want to trouble or rush Bernadette, even if he would have been more than happy for her to leave Michael and be all his. They have waited so long already, that a bit more time would not hurt anybody, but they had to do things properly. Then, there was her son, Samuel; he couldn't pretend he didn't exist and he knew Bernadette would never anything to cause him any harm even if she always avoided talking about Samuel with Shane. She loved and was proud of her son, but for some reason, every time Shane asked her about him, Bernadette always immediately changed the subject. Maybe she only wanted to keep him out of this mess for as long as she could, and Shane could understand it. He was prepared to give both their time. Bernadette stopped a minute in the hall and wondered whether she should drive up to Shane's or not. She tried to establish if there was more of a chance to be noticed on foot or with the car. If someone passed by, they would have spotted her anyway. She decided to walk. She entered the gate's code and as soon the gate opened enough to allow her to fit through, she went in. She opened the front door and called for Shane. Polly was the first to greet her with a defensive growl that soon became a welcoming bark, accompanied by an overexcited wag of her tail. Shane followed. He was wearing a pair of jeans and a white shirt left hanging outside his trousers. His hair was slightly too long to stay in a definite shape. He was different from Michael, who was so obsessed with keeping his hair in place and perfectly styled at all times. Bernadette felt an uncontrollable impulse to pass her fingers through his hair. They stopped for a second facing each other. They hadn't met after the funeral yet, but they both acknowledged that things were now on an entirely different level between them. Still, without saying a word, Bernadette threw her arms around his neck and let him hug her so tight that the air barely made it through her lungs. But she didn't feel any pain. She felt safe.

31

Bernadette looked at the man lying beside her and felt a sudden void in her stomach. She had to tell him the truth. They couldn't start a life together with that secret between them. And what if instead, it would have been Michael who revealed everything? Leaving him for Shane would destroy him, and she could just imagine him taking his revenge against them at any cost, regardless who else would have to pay the price. Shane told Bernadette about McCabe's visits and how he thought the sergeant started to suspect something. Bernadette had to admit that the whole idea of coming clean felt like it would be a relief, but unfortunately, she was also well aware of how it would look to the police: two former lovers back together, taking revenge on the one person who ruined their chance of having a life together. Shane saw that Bernadette's face had darkened and hugged her, whispering in her ear that everything would be all right. Would it be? Bernadette kept asking that question over and over as she was not sure that if after she told him the truth, he would want her again. They made love and stayed in bed nearly all morning. Shane had so many things he wanted to ask her but once again, it was not the right time—he could see that. They needed to leave Paul's affair behind them to have a fresh new start.

"Will I go to fix us some lunch?" Shane asked, caressing Bernadette face with his long fingers.

"I'll help you."

In the kitchen, Polly was patiently waiting for something to drop from the counter, and when this didn't happen, she went to lay under the table at the feet of her owner. The grey sky was contrasting with the yellow and the red of the leaves on the trees. Questions started to leave Shane's mouth before he realised it, but as always, when he wanted to talk about Samuel, Bernie froze and changed the subject. His interest was genuine and she started to realise how awkward her attitude might seem. Maybe it was time to tell. She held his hand in hers and started talking, determined to tell him what she was keeping from him, but as she started, the doorbell interrupted her. Shane stood up to go open the gate and retrieve his post. He was back in a few minutes, but Bernadette had lost her courage.

"So, what were you saying?" he asked, filling their glasses with more wine.

"Oh, nothing. I can't even remember. Probably nothing important."

It was mid-afternoon already, and Bernadette had done nothing at the house, nor had she walked Berta and Pedro, and probably was never going to. That evening, at The Snake, there was the annual table quiz to fundraise for the local sea guard association. She and Jane had booked a table for the four of them. The table quiz started at seven, so they agreed to meet there around six-thirty, meaning Michael was going to be home early and she had to go tidy up the house and herself as well. The last thing Bernadette wanted was to wash away Shane's smell from her body. After they made love, she could smell it all over her and just wanted to keep it on as long as she could. Bernadette didn't feel guilty towards Michael anymore. Instead, she felt guilty not feeling guilty. She could not wait to be able to walk in the daylight hand in hand with the love of her life. She so wanted to tell Jane and share her joy and excitement with her best friend, but it was too early. Too many things had to be sorted first. Then, the sudden sadness at the thought of Shane refusing her after she told him her secret, crept over her.

32

"Do we have to go to the damn table quiz this year, too?" Tim was driving and moaning with his wife.

"Of course, we have to, and if you will be good enough and try not to be too sarcastic, I might make you a nice surprise when we got home." Jane kissed her husband on the cheek, careful to not distract him from the road. Despite all those years together, Tim and Jane were as playful as teenagers. Things, of course, were not always paradisiacal in their marriage but over the last ten years, they had reconnected. Tim was not the only one upset about the night's plans. Dr Michael Greaney was even less happy about them, and he had his reasons as there was the danger that the alleged golf weekend would come up in conversation. He had thought to pretend of being sick, but not going could have been potentially more dangerous as Libbie was supposed to be there too with some ladies from her Pilates class. At least if he was there, he could keep an eye on both his wife and his mistress. He had discretely tried to talk Libbie into not going but what he obtained was the opposite effect: she lashed out one more time about how selfish he was and about how many sacrifices she was making for their love, while he was keeping up appearances with his wife. Michael remembered thinking, *Love? Our love? There is no such thing between us. It was supposed to be a brief flirt, and that was it. I don't love you; I fear you.* If only he could find the courage to say so! Dan had put away the comfy leather armchairs to make space for as many tables as he could. The annual table quiz he and Jerry had organised in support of the Local Coastal Guard for the last ten years, was about to start. Most of the participants rushed to the bar to get a drink before Dan stopped brewing beers. Everybody knew he had lost a brother in the sea and this was a cause particularly close to him. During the quiz, they didn't serve drinks and Dan usually just helped Jerry with reading the questions. When Libbie arrived, many heads turned and people began to whisper.

"Isn't that your widow, Billy?" George Polinsky asked, checking Libbie out from top to bottom.

"Yes, not much in distress, is she?" Billy knew his comment was not that professional but he also knew it was safe with George, who probably thought the same before salivating after those legs, which were exposed by a very short dress.

"Boys, please, no work and no chauvinist comments for the night." Martha intervened, raising her pint and inviting the two men to make a toast with her. "Use your clever brain for the quiz instead."

Everybody had taken their places, and Jerry was about to pick up the microphone and call for silence when Shane Flynn came in. He had bought a ticket, but all the tables were already completed with four persons. Dan quickly overlooked the room and spotted Martha and Billy at a table with only three participants, as Annette ditched them at the last minute for a date with some boy she had met online. When Detective Polinsky and Sergeant McCabe saw Dan coming towards their table with Shane, they looked at each other in a way that Martha only had learned to read over the years, and before they could do or say anything, she kicked them both under the table and threw them a scary look.

"Hope you don't mind if Shane joins you for the night, guys. All the tables are full and since you are the only in three..." Dan patted Shane on the back and left him there.

Billy couldn't hide his embarrassment, mainly after their last encounter and was not sure how exactly he was supposed to break the ice, but fortunately, his wife did it for him.

"Hi, Shane, I am Martha, Billy's wife. Very nice to meet you."

"The pleasure is all mine," Shane replied, shaking Martha's hand.

George Polinsky introduced himself too, while Billy was still silent until his wife kicked him again.

"Shane, nice to see you. It will be good to have an extra brain."

"You can't get enough of me, can you Billy?!"

Billy didn't reply but thought that in fairness, he deserved that. Before there was time for any other comments, Jerry called for everybody's attention and the quiz started. Dan declared a twenty-minutes break before starting the second round of questions and the reopening of the bar. Michael's phone buzzed and Libbie passed him as she headed outside for a cigarette. She wanted him to go up to her, and he was too afraid not to.

"If you will excuse me, I need the loo. Bernie, would you get me another beer, please, honey?" He didn't need another drink, but at least he was sure Bernadette wouldn't be wandering around looking for him, and judging by the queue at the bar, it would have to take the whole interval to get their drinks.

"I will get you both a drink, ladies, let me be your knight," Tim joked, mocking a bow in front of Jane and Bernadette, who had just spotted Shane going to the bar. This was her chance.

"No, no,"

The two lovers were now standing beside each other at the bar.

"Hi," Shane said, trying to sound as casual as possible.

"Hi," Bernadette replied. The look in her eyes needed no other words and their pretence to be simple acquaintances bumping into each other could only fool whoever was not looking straight at them. It was so hard for them both to not touch each other. Shane let Bernadette order before him in a chivalrous gesture and because the more time he spent away from McCabe and Polinsky, the better.

"You are beautiful," he whispered as she left to go back to her table. Bernadette smiled at him and tried not to drop the tray she was carrying. Jane was looking at her as she whispered something to Tim, and Bernadette wondered if she had noticed something. The guilt of lying to her best friend suddenly overwhelmed her.

"They would have made a fabulous couple," is what Jane had whispered to Tim.

"Well, honey, if it was not meant to be, it was not meant to be, and now we are all stuck with doctor pretty face and perfect hair." Tim raised his empty glass and pretended to toast to his wife, who always enjoyed his dark humour.

"Speaking of which, is it not taking him a bit too long?" Jane said, patting her husband's hand and kissing his bald head.

"Ah, he is probably combing his hair, making sure there is nothing out of place," Tim replied sarcastically and went on, "Anyway, I better go to the gents too, before the second round starts. I don't want to miss even a second of this exciting night."

Michael was still in the winter garden with Libbie but they were done. He quickly fixed his shirt back inside his trousers and walked back inside. He wanted to stop in the bathroom, but he saw Tim going in, so he went straight to the table hoping nobody saw them and that Libbie had not left any visible marks on him.

"And the winner is... Table number five! Congratulations," Martha instinctively gave a high-five to Shane who was sitting beside her.

"Now, before presenting the winners with their prize, I want to thank all of you for being here tonight and supporting the cause." In the general buzzing, Dan and Jerry went into the back to get the hamper for the winners. "Well, I think there is enough delicatessen for all of you. Enjoy and thanks again for your support." Dan and Jerry shook hands with Shane, Billy and George and hugged Martha.

"I will leave my share to your lovely wife, Billy. Nice to meet you again, Martha." Before Martha could thank him, Shane was gone.

"Well, honey, whatever you might think he had done, I don't think he did. He is too clever and kind. Good looking too, if I may say," Martha said to her husband jokingly.

"Oh, I don't want to get involved in this lovers' quarrel..." Detective Polinsky waved at Billy and kissed Martha on both cheeks, the Polish way.

Martha and Billy gathered their coats and their hamper and went toward the door where Bernadette was waiting for Michael to come back from the bathroom—for real this time. Bernadette saw them coming and turned her back to avoid them. She had nothing against either of them. On the contrary, she was quite fond of both, especially Martha, but with everything that was happening, she felt terribly uneasy around the sergeant. Bernadette and Martha had met a few years back through the book club they both were members of. The two women couldn't say they were friends, but they immediately liked each other and in normal circumstances, she would have been more than happy to stop by and have a chat with them. But now, the only thing she saw was the sergeant in charge of solving the murder she was in some way involved in. Also, she was sure that Billy had noticed Shane and her at the bar. Of course, it could be paranoia. Even when Libbie Mulligan passed by her earlier in the evening, she felt she had checked her out the same way she had at the funeral. Wholly absorbed in her thoughts, Bernadette didn't realise that Billy and Martha McCabe were now standing right behind her.

"Hello, Bernadette, how are you?" Martha gently pulled Bernadette's arm to attract her attention. Bernadette jumped and turned.

"Oh, dear, I didn't want to scare you," Martha went on.

"Oh, hi, no, I was just in my little word," Bernadette said, rushing to justify herself and hugged Martha. Billy was half-hidden behind the extravagant hamper he was clumsily holding and raised a few fingers to say hello, making sure to not drop the prize.

"Well done, guys, congratulations! And look at that hamper." Bernadette had regained some confidence and spotted Michael on his way to her.

"I know, isn't it amazing? And both Shane and George left me their share. Well, Mr Flynn offered first, and then I am afraid George had to do it to not look like a total boor."

Bernadette was glad that Shane's name came up before Michael joined them because she was sure her cheeks slightly blushed and hoped Billy McCabe had not noticed it.

"Well, we better go, or my husband will lose his arms holding that thing." Billy was already outside, and before stepping outside to meet him, Martha gave Bernadette a last glance, caressed the sleeve of her blouse and said, "Your blouse is gorgeous, I have been admiring it all evening." Bernadette looked down at the front of her top.

"Ah thank you, Martha."

With Billy struggling with the hamper outside, the women said goodbye and Martha walked out. Bernadette had not picked that blouse randomly. It was the blouse she was wearing the first time Shane had seen her after moving back.

He told her during one of their coffee encounters at Maude's that she looked as sparkling as the sequins. She had worn it to look sparkling for him tonight.

"Jeez Martha, you can be a chatterbox", the sergeant said to his wife when she eventually got into the car with him.

"I know, and that is why you love me, and if you are wondering what to give me for my birthday, I might suggest a blouse like that—with golden sequins."

Billy was tired and in a hurry to get home because he knew he was probably slightly over the alcohol limit, like the rest of the village. He was not listening to his wife, but something she said captured his unconscious attention.

"What? What did you say?"

"I knew you were not listening to me, honey, and I will only repeat it because that could be my birthday present, we are talking about, you know..."

Billy was not interested in getting ideas for his wife's birthday. His focus was on the sequins that looked precisely like the one Annette found in Shane's bedroom. Suddenly, he had a flash of Bernadette and Shane talking at the graveyard and tonight, ignoring each other instead. He thought of the two wine glasses in Shane's living room and tried to remember if Bernadette was wearing lipstick tonight and what colour she had on. He could have asked Martha, but he was not ready to share his thoughts yet—not even with his wife. He had to be sure that the dots he started to connect created in the right shape.

33

"Annette!" Billy McCabe barked from his office.

"Yes, boss, sir. Do you need me?"

"No Annette, I just called because I particularly like the sound of your name."

The sergeant is having a dreadful day, Annette thought. Martha had probably put him on a low carb, low sugar, low protein diet again but still, the way he was talking to her was not right. She stood there, in front of his desk, with an angry look on her face, waiting for his instructions. Billy knew he had been unfair to his deputy, but he had more important matters to deal with at the moment. In fact, after the quiz night, he could not stop thinking about Bernadette and Shane. He mentally went through everything he knew and despite the forensic evidence pointing away from the two former lovers, every else led back to them. They had the motive and the time and neither of them had an alibi that could have been corroborated by someone else. Billy read their statements once again. They were both at home alone, never left the house the whole day, and neither of them heard anything. He had asked Martha if there was any gossip in the village about Bernadette and Shane being more than friends, but she was not of any help. Instead, she informed him that actually, the most popular rumour was about Michael allegedly having an affair. Billy McCabe was not surprised, the doctor had an ego the size of a cruise ship and that brand-new fancy two-seater car he had, clearly stated he was a man in full middle-age crisis. Unfortunately, being unfaithful was not a crime, and Dr Greaney could have been guilty of a lack of morals but not of murder. If the victim was Shane, maybe he could have had raised some suspicions, but for this investigation, the doctor was entirely irrelevant.

"Boss?" Annette called out after standing there for five minutes while the sergeant sat absorbed in his thoughts. "Yes, Annette, do you remember what Mrs Hazel said when she came to collect her passport?"

"That she needed to go to visit her sister in Spain," Annette replied, looking at her boss bewildered.

"Not that, Annette," he snapped.

How Annette could be so clever and so clueless at the same time baffled him.

"I am talking about what she said about the village going mad and even good people turning bad. Annette, do you remember?"

A couple of days after the murder, Mrs Hazel went to the station to collect her renewed passport and she could not stop talking about the latest happenings. She then started to complain about the village gradually turning into a big town where people were not kind to each other anymore, even the ones who always had been. Eventually, a sparkle appeared in the young guard's eyes. "Are you thinking what I am thinking?" "I think I do, sir, and after what you told me about the quiz night and the graveyard, it does raise some suspicions. But we don't know it was the day of the finding. Mrs Hazel hasn't said."

"But we can go back and ask, and hopefully, her memory won't betray her."

That very same afternoon, Billy McCabe showed up at Mrs Hazel's doorstep.

"Oh, Billy, dear, what a surprise. Please, come in," Mrs Hazel escorted her guest to the sitting room and offered him a seat on the green velvet couch.

Still, now that he was an adult, Billy felt under examination whenever he was in front of his former primary school teacher. Billy sat down, took his hat off out of respect, and started nervously to play with it. Mrs Hazel sat on the other end of the couch to study the sergeant.

"Still nervous in front of your old teacher, Billy? Really? You know that I should be the one who should be nervous in front of you? The chief of Seacross police. I always knew you would follow in your father's footsteps."

Billy smiled, and in doing so, he felt his face blush. Mrs Hazel gave him a quick pat on the knee and stood up, "I'll tell you what, dear, I am going to make us some tea and then you will tell me why you are here."

The house was silent; the only noises Billy could hear was the kettle boiling in the kitchen and Mrs Hazel getting the tray to serve the tea ready. She appeared back in the sitting room carrying a silver tray which held a china tea set and a plate of biscuits. Her hands were slightly shaking and the sergeant got up to help.

"Oh, thank you, Billy. The tray is heavier than I thought, and my hands and balance are not as steady as they used to be."

Billy laid the tray on the coffee table in front of the sofa and they both sat back.

"Before you start, let me tell you something. If you are here for that ticket I refused to pay to Annette, you can save your time and mine. I am not going to pay for it."

Before the old woman could finish, Billy raised his hands to stop her, "I'm not here for that, Mrs Hazel. Don't worry."

Happy that her principles and motivation had been heard, Mrs Hazel poured the tea into the cups and started blowing on hers to cool it down. Sergeant McCabe was not sure how to start the conversation; he didn't want to reveal his suspects, so he had to find a way to "interrogate" the old lady without saying too much.

"Mrs Hazel, I know it might sound strange, and I can't say why I am asking, but do you remember the day you came to the station to collect your passport?"

"Of course, I do. I can still remember what I ate for breakfast, you know?"

Billy felt mortified, "I know, and I didn't mean to say that, of course..."

"It's ok, Billy, now please go on and ask whatever you need to as I am sure you don't have the whole day to stay here chatting and drinking tea with me, and in total honesty, neither do I."

Glad that the old teacher put him out of his misery and opened the way to him to ask whatever he needed to, Billy enquired about what she saw on the day of the finding.

"Mrs Hazel, you were upset for what was going on in the village and how people had suddenly become rude, and you mentioned a neighbour of yours. I need to know who it was and when it happened."

The old teacher placed her cup back onto the saucer and took one of the biscuits. Her sharp small lively eyes were fixed on the sergeant, while she tried to remember what he was precisely referring to and at the same time, hiding the fact that her memory was maybe not as good as she publicised.

"Oh, yes, I remember. I had a very upsetting day. The incompetent new postman misdelivered my parcel. He left it at the new house down the hill, the one they had finished building, you know?" Mrs Hazel waited for Billy to nod his understanding before she went on, "Apparently, they had a similar surname to mine, but that is not an acceptable excuse. However, what upset me most was his lack of apologies when the following morning I told him what he did." Mrs Hazel rolled her eyes and shook her head to add emphasis to her story, "Anyway, when I got home that afternoon, I found a note on my door from the people who had received my parcel. Very decent people, I must say, and they were kind enough to come up here and deliver it back to me. Unfortunately, I was not home, so they left a note. I always go to the hairdresser on Wednesday afternoons—it is a tranquil day at the salon. You don't get out with your head sore because of the bickering."

Billy had no interest either in the woman's digression or her hair routine, but he was aware he could not interrupt her and had to let her talk. Mrs Hazel drunk another sip of tea, "Now, where was I? Oh, yes then, I went straight away to get my parcel and when I came back, I saw Bernadette rushing home." She eventually got to what Billy wanted to hear.

"And you are sure it was her, and it was the day of the murder?"

"Well, young man, as I already said, my memory and sight are still good. She didn't turn her head to say hello, but I know it was her. Besides, she was in front of her gate, scrambling with her keys. As for the day, I am pretty sure it was the day they found Paul dead because after I saw it on the evening news, I remember thinking it was such an unfortunate day: the parcel, the murder, and my most lovely neighbour having turned suddenly rude." Mrs Hazel took another biscuit to dip into her tea. A smile appeared on Billy's face as pieces of this mystery were finally starting to fit together.

34

Michael knew that the night of the quiz, he and Libbie took it too far, and the worst part was that she liked it. In the immediate days after their little rendezvous at the pub, he tried his best not to see her, but now he was running out of excuses, and she was pressing him. The phone was constantly ringing or buzzing. He finally agreed to meet at her place, with the excuse of a particularly busy day at the office. He didn't stay long but enough to make her happy. He needed to keep her quiet a little longer and, in the meantime, would need to think of something to get him out of this situation. The problem was that whatever he would do, it would come back like a boomerang and hit him. Libbie would never let him go without a fight, and ultimately make him pay. Bernadette didn't seem to notice how absent and tense her husband was and for Michael, that was simply something to be grateful for rather than worried. It never crossed his mind that it could be a sign that something was going on in Bernadette's life too. He was so absorbed in trying to conceal his wrongdoing, that he hadn't noticed his wife's distance. The only thing he noticed was that she seemed happier and content and believed it could only be to his advantage when he would eventually have to tell her the truth about his affair. Their life was perfect, and she wouldn't want to throw it away for one single mistake he made. Bernadette would never have to know that Libbie was only the last of his many mistakes. Of course, he considered the possibility of Libbie spilling the beans but then, it would be the word of an abandoned and angry mistress against his. As much as Bernadette knew he had never let her down over the years, starting from their beginning together when once he knew the truth about her, he would have been so easy for him to turn his back and build a more comfortable life for himself. Michael planned to keep Libbie at bay and as far from his wife as possible until he found the right moment to speak to Bernadette. It would be hard on their marriage, but he was sure it wouldn't destroy it. Michael couldn't say if he were still in love with his wife, but he knew he still wanted to be married to her. He liked their life together; he liked the family they created and didn't want to lose it as much as he didn't want to lose the clinic and half of his assets. Michael would reason with his wife and would beg to be forgiven for the sake of a life together that could still be a happy one. As mean as it could sound, Michael would remind Bernadette that she owed him a debt of gratitude, and he was going to use it if he had to. The two of them were the only ones who knew a truth that could hurt their family to an extent far too significant than a meaningless affair. Bernadette would never jeopardise Samuel's happiness and trust. A divorce would cost Michael the clinic and half of his assets, but it would potentially cost Bernadette much more. When Shane Flynn moved back, Michael worried what kind of impact it would have on his wife and them. He couldn't deny that the feeling of being Bernadette's second choice came back. At the beginning of their story, the ghost of Shane had haunted him for months, and he wondered what she felt for him: was it love, or was he just a comfortable parachute she found at the right time before she had fallen too low? Then, gradually, all his doubts vanished. They built a successful life together and Bernadette never made him doubt her commitment to them as a couple and as a family. Michael never asked his wife how she felt seeing Shane Flynn again, or what it was like to have him live so close. His wife, on the other hand, never spoke a word about the return of her first undiscussed love. As far as Michael was concerned, Shane and Bernadette no longer had anything to do one with one another, and the night of the table quiz proved he had no reason to be concerned. The two former lovers barely talked to each other. The logic behind his sudden concern about Shane and Bernadette was not jealousy or fear, but it was merely about the possibility that after hearing of his affair, Bernadette would go crying to Shane Flynn.

"Darling, are you here with me?" Michael's mind was preoccupied, and he hoped Libbie wouldn't ask him anything she had just said. Michael looked at his wristwatch and got up. "I am sorry, honey, but I have to go now. The clinic will be hectic this afternoon." Libbie followed him to the door,"I was thinking that since as you are working so much lately, maybe we could go away for another weekend?" Michael just smiled at Libbie as he let her fix his tie. He didn't want to argue with her, and he didn't need to because he was going to put their story to an end well before any weekend away could ever happen.

"Yes, that sounds great. Just give me the time to organise myself." Michael immediately noticed that his straight "yes" was now obscured by having mentioned that he had to deal with his wife before making any plans. He could already feel one of her rants coming one, so before she could even start moaning and complaining, Michael kissed her on the forehead and reassured her.

"Come on, honey, you know I need to sort things out with Bernadette first. But you know what? Things will change sooner than you expect. You start searching for a nice place to go to." He kissed his mistress on the forehead and left. Libbie closed the door behind her and ran to the living room window overlooking the parking lot to see Michael get in the car and leave. He looked up at her and waved. They both knew that would be one of their last secret encounters, and they both smiled but for many different reasons. Libbie poured herself a cup of tea and started to surf the web for short city breaks across Europe—this time, they deserved a real weekend away. She set her mind on Budapest. It was considered expensive, but they could afford it. A happy smile appeared on her pretty young face at the thought of "they". Soon, they could be a couple in daylight. Still smiling, she went to take a shower and change. Ever since she was a little girl, Libbie knew what she wanted for her life: a man capable of protecting and supporting her as she deserved. "Two hearts and a shack" was something she had never believed in. She saw how financial difficulties destroyed her parents' marriage and made her an unhappy child, continually feeling inadequate. Love doesn't put a meal on the table and doesn't win against the day-to-day struggle when you have no money to pay the bills. But thanks to Michael, she was going back to being a queen. She could imagine how the village gossipers would no longer be able to look down on her. They could still whisper behind her back, but they would have to respect her—the new Mrs Greaney. She would be a pillar of the community, along with her husband. She opened her wardrobe and stared at her outfits from her London days; they would soon go out again. Libbie picked out an emerald green cocktail dress still in the launderette wrapping. Sure, it was of no use with Paul but with Michael, she planned on wearing it even when they dined at home. The image of Michael and Bernadette's impressive house materialised in her mind and she pictured herself making coffee in the winter mornings wrapped in a cashmere gown, or gardening in the summer in a perfect-fitting Laura Ashley flower-print dress. Her future was happy and wealthy, and she was dreaming of it until the thought of Bernadette fighting to keep Michael and the house, and it made her smile vanish. She thought of Bernadette pathetically fighting for her husband and refusing to accept he had ditched her for someone younger and prettier. She would claim the house for the sake of their son, and with no dignity left, she would play the victim—women always do that, especially the older ones who have nothing left but call for revenge on their husbands. Poor Michael, Libbie thought, he had to prepare to battle, but she would be by his side all the way.

35

Bernadette was driving home when she saw Billy McCabe leaving Mrs Hazel's house. At first, she was worried that something happened to her lovely old neighbour, but then, Shane's words about Billy getting close to them was echoing in her head and even more worrying thoughts started to haunt her. The day of the finding, Mrs Hazel saw her running outside on her way back from Shane's house. Bernadette had to know why Sgt McCabe was at Mrs Hazel, and what she'd told him. Bernadette hadn't spoken to Mrs Hazel since that day, and maybe now it was time she went and apologised for her behaviour. She reversed and sped back to the village to pick up an apple pie to bring over to her neighbour. With the excuse to check on her and apologise, she hoped to find out what Billy wanted from her.

"Here, dear, have a seat and I will be back with some tea." Mrs Hazel didn't seem upset about Bernadette's behaviour from the last time they saw each other.

"It's very nice of you to come here and check on me, and you shouldn't have brought anything, really, there was no need."

"No bother, Mrs Hazel. Besides, considering the police were up here, I kind of got worried something happened and I just wanted to be sure you were all right."

"As I said, Bernadette, I am fine, and you are the sweetest neighbour."

Before Mrs. Hazel could say anything else, Bernadette took her chance to question her.

"Well, you know, to be totally honest, I also wanted to apologise for being so rude last time we saw each other." Mrs. Hazel said nothing, so Bernadette continued. "Do you remember outside my gate? I had a nasty headache and I couldn't wait to go home and lay down. I didn't mean to be rude to you or anything..."

This time, Mrs. Hazel perceived her embarrassment and with a big smile, touched her hand and reassured her it was fine. "Everybody has bad days. It is just that it was a bit of a crazy bad day for me too." Mrs Hazel began to tell the story of the parcel when she suddenly stopped. "You know, Bernadette, it is amusing that you brought this up just now." Bernadette cocked her head and looked at the old woman with a bewildered expression that clearly suggested she go on with whatever she was saying. "As I was saying, dear, Billy McCabe was here to talk about the exact same thing a short while ago too. What a coincidence!"

There was no coincidence, Bernadette thought, while her heart started to race. Mrs Hazel spooned up another piece of pie and looked at her guest in contempt. She had no intention to voluntary reveal any other details of her conversation with the sergeant. Bernadette had to make the next move.

"So, did McCabe say why he was inquiring about the day of the murder again? I thought he had already taken statements from the neighbourhood."

Mrs Hazel poured both of them more tea and holding her cup in the air for a few seconds, took a sip and with an absorbed expression said, "To be honest, dear, I wondered the same. Moreover, the thing that left me even more puzzled was his interest in knowing again if I saw someone on the road, and I told him I didn't expect you, of course." Bernadette's hands started to shake so much she had to put her cup down in the fear it would have slipped off her fingers. She looked at her watch and, pretending she was late for something, she left. As soon Bernadette was out of Mrs Hazel's little pedestrian gate, she took out her mobile from the pocket of her jacket and started to type: *I need to see you. ASAP.* A few hours passed and Shane had yet to reply. Bernadette felt like she was going mad. He always replied to her texts immediately. Something was wrong! Catastrophic scenarios of herself and Shane being questioned and ultimately arrested for a crime they didn't commit were filling her head. Her life, her dream of a family, everything would be destroyed. She kept standing at the kitchen window, staring at her garden covered by a carpet of yellow and red leaves. An autumn landscape that would have usually relaxed her, but not today. Bernadette knew there were no new texts because she had not heard the alert, but she impulsively kept checking her screen. She couldn't bear the uncertainty any longer; she grabbed the house key to go to Shane's and try to find out what was going on, when she noticed the gate light flashing. Michael was at home. Bernadette dropped the keys back into the bowl on the console by the door and ran to the bathroom to check her face. She was sure her makeup was smudged and that her mascara had left black lines under her eyes. Ever since she was a little girl, whenever Bernadette was anxious, nervous, or angry, she cried. Michael always thought it was a sign of her compassionate nature, but it was not. It was nothing but a nervous reaction. She rarely cried when in pain. She touched up her make up with the few spare products she always kept in the downstairs bathroom. Her phone was still silent and her hands still shaky. "Breathe in and breathe out, Bernie, everything is going to be fine," she said, but those words could not even fool her.

36

Michael stepped into the house and was welcomed by Berta and Pedro. He petted the two dogs and called for his wife. The car was in the driveway, and the door was not locked—she had to be home. When she didn't answer, he went outside in the greenhouse to see if she was there, but there was no trace of her in there either.

Bernadette had heard him, but she locked herself in the bathroom for a few more minutes in the hope of receiving an answer from Shane, but her mobile stayed silent. Michael called for her again, and she could no longer pretend she had not heard him.

"Hey, here you are! Did you not hear me calling for you?"

"No, actually, I was in the bathroom. How was your day?"

"The usual. You want a glass?" Bernadette thanked her husband and took a long sip of her cabernet. Hopefully, it would help her relax.

"If you want to go and take a shower, it will take another while for dinner to be ready as I just started it. I had an afternoon tea with Mrs Hazel, and you know how much of a chatterbox she can be."

"Why, did something happened?" Michael asked, curious about why his wife had spent her afternoon with their grumpy old neighbour. No matter how nice Bernadette always said she was, to him, Mrs Hazel had never looked that nice and cheerful.

Yes, just I don't know the fucking extent of what happened because my lover wouldn't answer my texts and phone calls, were the words screaming inside Bernadette's head.

"No, just out of courtesy. Mrs Hazel is a lovely lady, and she has nobody left," she said instead.

"If you say so, she is never that lovely with me, though," Michael said, emptying his glass and grabbing a cheese cracker from the cupboard.

"That is why you made her spend a fortune for her dentures," Bernadette replied, attempting a joke with the intent to look and sound as normal as possible.

Michael shrugged his shoulders and went upstairs to take a shower. Halfway up the stairs, he remembered he left his mobile in the kitchen and not on silent mode. Recently, Libbie had started to text him and sometimes even called him if she knew he was at home with Bernadette. He tried to tell her not to, but the conversation ended in Libbie having the usual tantrum about her miserable role as a mistress. Michael quickly went back to the kitchen and grabbed the phone. He immediately put it on silent and eventually went for his shower. As he predicted, Libbie texted him and after not receiving an immediate answer, she tried to ring him. He knew better than to ignore her calls, and after making sure Bernadette was still in the kitchen, he closed the bedroom door and called his mistress back.

"I stopped by the clinic, but you already left. I thought you were working late." Libbie's tone had a deceptive sweetness that failed to hide the inquisition behind her question. Michael stayed silent, wondering what to answer.

"Yea, that was what I thought too but the last two patients cancelled," he finally said. Libbie seemed to believe him and hung up, extorting the promise that they would have lunch together the following day. Michael wondered if that night would be a good night to come clean with his wife. He knew that rationally, no night would be a good one, so he just needed to decide, collect his courage and talk to her. Downstairs, Bernadette had her mobile on silent mode, but she kept it in the pocket of her apron. Still, there was no answer from Shane. She thought of inventing some excuse to leave the house and go check on him, but she couldn't come up with anything credible at that time in the evening. She heard Michael's steps coming down the stairs and she quickly checked her phone one last time. Still no news from Shane. Over dinner, Michael was more talkative than he had been in recent months. He simply wanted to attract his wife's interest and put her at ease as he had made his decision: tonight, he would tell her. Then, tomorrow he would end his story with Libbie. Unfortunately, the evening went far differently from what Michael had planned as Bernadette was absent, and all the attention from her husband was just annoying her. The only thing she wanted was to get up and check her phone. She wished that damn thing would buzz in her pocket, and she wanted to see Shane's name on display. Michael took his wife's hand and opened his mouth to start talking, to start introducing that he had something to tell her—something important. Upstairs in the bedroom, he had prepared his speech and now was the moment. However, before he could say anything, Bernadette rushed from the room to the bathroom. The food she had eaten turned Bernadette's stomach and she felt ill. She locked the door behind her and turned on the sink, trembling. Michael ran after her and knocked on the door. "Bernadette, what's wrong? Are you ok?" He was upset because his plan was ruined but he was also genuinely concerned for his wife.

"I am fine, just feeling sick." After a few minutes, she came out, her eyes red. Her stomach was torn in cramps and she had cried, but not because she was sick, but because the phone eventually buzzed with an incoming text from Shane: *I know. Billy just left.*

37

Bernadette had a sleepless night, and she pretended to be asleep every time Michael tried to approach her to ask how she felt.

She continued this pretence until morning and only got up when he left for work. As unfair as it was, she couldn't deal with his questions. She could not cope with him anymore, but there was nothing she could say or do until she knew what was happening and what McCabe knew of the situation. With Shane reaching out to her and their appointment to see each other, she felt better already –it was just a pity her stomach didn't feel the same relief and kept rejecting food. Bernadette threw her half-eaten toast in the bin and went to take a shower. The redness in her eyes was still there; she would need to wear extra makeup. There was so much going on in her head at that moment; still, there was room for some vanity. She refused to show up at her lover's with a crappy face. She gave Pedro and Berta two digestive biscuits, a real treat to ease her guilt for not walking them again. "Sorry, guys. Behave, yea?" She had always felt stupid ordering the dogs whenever she left the house, but it was a habit that proved impossible to stop. It had all started when Samuel was a child, and he played big brother to their first dog. "Now, Lucky," he would say, "we are going out, but you be a good boy, ok?" Her son's voice as a child resonated in Bernadette's head. She looked at herself briefly in the mirror before opening the front door, and she felt a shiver of shame thinking of Samuel and thinking of what she was doing to her family, and what would be left of it when everything was over. Bernadette walked as fast as she could to Shane's house.

Shane opened the front door and without saying a word, he hugged her tight.

"What did Billy want from you? What did he say? You know he went to speak to Mrs Hazel, right? Billy knows I was not home that day," spewed Bernadette, with her head still buried in Shane's chest. He gently lifted her face toward his and wiped the tears away. She felt so small and lost in his arms. She was scared but felt safe at the same time, if it was even possible. It was as though nothing bad could happen to her when Shane held her, but the thought of his reaction when she would tell him the truth stiffened her body. Would he still want to stay with her? She shook her head to shake the thoughts away. *Now was not the time to worry about that – there were other things to worry about*, she thought to herself. They walked into the living room and sat on the sofa.

"Billy came here last night, saying he knows something is going on between us and that it was time for me to come clean. He said he knows we are involved in Paul's murder."

Shane gave Bernadette the full account of his meeting with Billy. Bernadette listened silently, covering her mouth with her hand and fighting with all her strength the urge to break into tears. She turned pale, and her eyes widened and screamed of fear. Shane took her hands in his and reassured her, "I don't think he can prove any of his claims. Otherwise, I would already be at the station."

Though that was supposed to make Bernadette feel better, it didn't. She got up and moved toward the window, her gaze upon the garden. She looked, but she could not see anything.

"What are we to do?" asked Bernadette, with her back to Shane. "He won't stop chasing us until he discovers what truly happened. We shouldn't have lied from the beginning." She turned to face him. He couldn't hide his surprise and pain at hearing her words. Bernadette realised immediately how harsh she had sounded. It was true he had been the one who didn't want to call the police and reveal what had truly happened, but he had for good reasons—reasons she agreed with, too. Bernadette went back to the couch where Shane was still sitting and kneeled in front of him. She rested her head on his lap; they both stayed still and silent for a few seconds until Shane started to caress her hair gently. She didn't want to place the blame on him; she was only scared. Bernadette stood up. She looked down at Shane and kissed him. She lost herself in that kiss, and all her worries disappeared at the touch of his skin on hers. They made love, and everything else no longer mattered and ceased to exist.

"I have to go now,"said Bernadette reluctantly. She would have never left that bed, but she wanted to go home in case Michael had called to check on her.

They kissed one last time. "Tell me that everything is going to be ok," she said, with eyes begging for assurance.

"I promise." That was enough for her.

“Morning, boss,” greeted Annette. Billy waved at her and went to his office, closing the door behind him. Just as he was getting himself comfortable and settled, Annette knocked at the door and without waiting for the sergeant’s answer, she came in and handed him his mug of coffee. She then took a seat across his desk.

“So? How did it go?” she asked. Her curious little green eyes were fixed on Billy, who knew precisely what she was after but enjoyed teasing his deputy. He took a sip of his coffee slowly and looked at Annette with a baffled expression, pretending he didn’t know what she was referring.

“Come on, chief…”

Annette knew her boss liked to mock her, but she also knew he trusted her enough to keep her in the loop regarding the investigation. The advantage of working in such a small station was that they were still involved in everything that was happening in all cases, even if they weren’t your own.

“I am telling you, Annette. I still don’t know how, but I am positive the two of them are involved in Paul’s murder in some way. Of course, he denied everything, starting with his affair with Mrs Greaney. But he is a liar—that is as true as me sitting right here in front of you right now.”

“Have you shown him the sequin?” Annette asked excitedly, still proud of being the one to find the single piece of evidence to break their case potentially.

“No, I didn’t, Annette. What for? To have the man laugh at me, as half the village likely possess a jumper like that—my wife included, who just bought one of the same kind?”

Annette refused to be discouraged and could not believe the resigned attitude of her boss. "But we have an eyewitness who saw Bernadette emerging from his house right after the homicide."

"No, Annette. We have an eyewitness who saw Bernadette walking home. We only concluded that she was coming from Shane's house."

"Damn it. There must be a way."

Billy drank what was left of his coffee and stayed quiet, thinking for a few minutes. Annette knew that expression well; he was plotting something.

"Maybe we should also pay Mrs Greaney a visit and hear what she has to say."

Twenty minutes later, after Sergeant McCabe had stopped at Maude's for a fruit scone, he made his way to Green Hills once more. He pulled over in front of the Greaneys' residence and swallowed the last bite of his scone, which was barely visible under the mountain of cream and jam he had spread on top of it. After checking for food residue on his face, the sergeant got out of the car and rang the bell at the gate, but no one answered. Through the hedges that surrounded the house, he could see Bernadette's car. If she wasn't home, she couldn't be far. He suspected where she might be. Billy thought of calling Shane to see if his instinct was right, but he had no excuse for the call this time and was risking a lawsuit for harassment. He turned the car around and drove back to the village. He stopped for petrol and called Annette to give her an update.

"Shit, I bet she was at home but didn't want to talk to you."

Maybe Annette was right, and that game of cat and mouse was not leading them anywhere.

"You know, Annette. I think it's time to start tightening the rope around their necks. Put a bit of pressure on them, because whatever it is they are hiding could be crucial for the investigation. And I know exactly how to do it," said Billy confidently. "I will see you at the station in half an hour."

"Right, sir," Billy already had his index finger on the red button to hang up when he heard Annette still talking.

"Sir, are you still there? I forgot that Detective Polinsky called asking for you."

"Oh, ok. And did you take a message?"

"Yes!"

"Well, Annette, what did he say, for fuck's sake? Do I have to pull the words out of your mouth?" Billy was losing his patience already, and a call from Polinsky could only mean that someone above him wanted updates, which he had none to give at that moment—at least, none that could be supported by evidence.

"He said to ring him back with some updates, as the deputy chief is starting to get anxious." Billy hung up. He would have to take care of that later; for now, he had to pay someone else a visit.

38

Billy McCabe parked outside Michael Greaney's dental clinic and went in.

"Good morning, chief, how can we help you?" Sally greeted him with a big smile.

"Good morning, Sally is the doc in today? I need to talk to him."

Sally cocked her head and looked at the chief, but before she could say anything, Billy specified he was not there for their professional services. That was enough for Sally not to ask anything further. "Oh, ok, chief. Well, he is with a patient at the moment, but it shouldn't take long. Do you want to take a seat while you wait?"

"Thank you, Sally." Billy removed his hat and went to the adjacent waiting room.

Around ten minutes later, Michael materialised in front of Sally, along with his patient.

"Mr Parrot had just had a little adjustment on his dentures, Sally." Sally knew precisely how much to charge poor Mr Parrot.

Before Michael went back to his room, Sally excused herself for a moment and reached the doctor.

"Doctor Greaney, Chief McCabe is in the waiting room. He wants to talk to you."

From the look on Michael's face, it was obvious he had no idea what Billy McCabe wanted from him, that was not professionally related.

Since Mr Parrot was the last patient of the morning, Michael told Sally to take her break, and he went to the waiting room where Billy had comfortably collapsed onto one of the armchairs with the latest issue of the Reader's Digest in his hands. Michael's confidence always struck Billy as something artificial and cocky, and as they shook hands, the sergeant imagined the pretty dentist practicing his cool attitude in front of the mirror as a daily routine before leaving home. With his slim toned figure, perfect hair and excellent style, Michael reminded Billy of one of those American soap opera characters. Martha shared his opinion on Michael, but just for the fun of teasing her husband, she used to remind him that he was a show-off indeed, but with a damn flat stomach. Billy instinctively looked down at his round waist, before speaking to the dentist whose expression was of obvious curiosity about the reason for the sergeant's visit.

"Nothing really to worry about, Doc. I'm here because I was hoping to talk again with your wife, about the day of the murder, you know, as a witness," Billy stopped for a few seconds to give Michael time to absorb what he was saying.

He wanted to see if he would have some reaction but the dentist's expression stayed imperturbable.

"I stopped by your house this morning..." Billy went on, "...but nobody answered the door or the phone, and because I don't have Mrs Greaney's mobile, I thought to stop by and ask you to tell her to come down to the station at her earliest convenience, of course."

Eventually, Michael's expression changed to that of surprise. "I don't understand," Michael's tone was hesitant, "she has been sick since last night. She must have been home. Maybe she was in the bathroom and had not heard the bell. Did you try to ring at home?"

"Yes, as I just said, otherwise I wouldn't be here, would I?"

"Right, yes, of course, you said that before. Sorry, but I am a bit confused and worried also. Maybe something happened to Bernadette, but... in that case, I would have been informed, would I not? Never mind, chief, I don't know what to say, ... I am just an old worrywart."

Michael's confidence was gradually fading away word after word, and McCabe had to admit that he was enjoying it. He knew he was pushing the situation, but he had no other choice.

"I wouldn't be worried, Doc. You are probably right, and she was probably just in the bathroom when I rang."

Michael looked at Billy and wanted to believe his words but was incapable of relaxing and couldn't stop worrying. The bomb was dropped and Michael looked sincerely surprised that his sick wife was not at home. Billy knew that when Michael would question her and tell her about his visit, she would feel the pressure, exactly how sergeant Billy McCabe wanted. The only way he could get something out of Bernadette and Shane was to make them feel hunted, and Michael would be of great help without even realising it. It was an unfair game, but it was his only chance to throw some light on the case.

"Ok, Doc, I think I took too much of your time now. Thanks for your collaboration and I will expect Bernadette at the station as soon she is available."

Billy shook the hand of a very distracted Michael and left. Michael locked the clinic door behind the chief and went to the reception desk to call Bernadette. She was not answering the landline or her mobile. He didn't know what to think. That morning, Michael had left his wife sick in bed and didn't expect her to be out just a few hours later unless she went to the doctor. That could be a reasonable explanation: she was unreachable because she was at the doctor. He waited another ten minutes and tried to ring Bernadette again, still no answer. Now, he was starting to become concerned. If she was at home, she could not keep missing the phone, and if she was out, she had her mobile with her. Even if she had left her phone behind, she should have been back home by now. Michael removed his scrubs, grabbed his jacket and car keys and headed home. He was sure that there was a straightforward explanation for his wife's unavailability. But what if she felt sick and had fainted, and couldn't ask for help? He was better off checking. Michael tried to ring Bernadette one more time but again nobody answered at the other end of the line. He left a voicemail saying he couldn't reach her and was going home. He tried to keep his voice calm and not to sound alarmed or suspicious about her whereabouts, in case she was perfectly fine, and nothing happened. Michael didn't want to make her feel suffocated; he knew it was a feeling she always hated and now, more than ever, he needed her on his side as he had decided to confess his betrayal. Bernadette's car was in the driveway as the chief said, and Berta and Pedro were out in the garden. Bernadette never left the house with the dogs out. Michael didn't know if it was a good or a bad sign. She could be in bed profoundly asleep or the shower or even the greenhouse if she was feeling better, or she could be lying unconscious somewhere in the house. Michael slipped the key in the door lock only to discover that the door was ajar. He went in and called for his wife, hardly concealing his alarmed tone.

"In the kitchen..." Bernadette's tone was instead relaxed and cheerful.

Michael stopped a minute in the hall, thinking about how to tackle this: will he pretend nothing happened or will he inquire about why she was not answering either the door or the phone?

"I am sorry, I slept through most of the morning and when I woke up, I felt much better and went out to the greenhouse. I left my phone inside and only saw your calls and voicemail when I came back inside, literally ten minutes ago."

Bernadette's explanation was perfectly plausible, and Michael didn't think anything about it.

"Well, it's better this way. I'm glad you are feeling better." Michael gave his wife a kiss and went to wash his hands. Bernadette's uncontrollable reaction was to stiffen, but her husband didn't notice. A few months ago, she would have been the happiest woman in the world to have this kind of attention from her husband but now, she didn't want it anymore, not from him. The closer he came to her, the more afraid she became that he could smell Shane on her. Bernadette still had not turned to face her husband. She was too scared that he could read the lies on her face. She had put her phone in silent mode while she was at Shane's and only saw Michael's calls when she got back home. He was going home, and she barely had time to think of an excuse or have a shower. Michael went back into the kitchen and sat at the already-set table, while Bernadette served the two of them some soup. Michael wondered for a minute whether this was the perfect time to talk to his wife, but then Billy McCabe came to his mind. In the mayhem, he forgot about him. He had to tell Bernadette to go see him at the station first thing in the morning.

39

To Libbie, that day was the start of a new chapter in her story with Michael. He was supposed to talk to Bernadette the previous night, and today, they were going out for lunch, eventually like an ordinary couple. Today's lunch represented a new beginning for Libbie, and it had to be celebrated in style. She picked out of her outfits that emerald cocktail dress she was trying on a few days earlier. She left well in advance with the intention to get to the restaurant a bit early to be sure to have the best table: possibly private and by the window. The place was a twenty minutes' drive out of town, and Libbie completely understood that Michael didn't want to go anywhere too local just yet, and it honestly didn't matter to her since he had finally made his choice: he had chosen her over his wife. She only wished the place was closer because her heels, although beautiful and sexy, were also the most uncomfortable to drive in. Libbie kept checking her watch. She had now been sitting at the table alone for over an hour. It was quite clear that Michael was not going to show up. Her rage was hard to control but she refused to believe he ditched her. *Maybe something happened to him,* she thought, and a wave of guilt ran through her for getting so angry. That it was not what a good wife would do. She tried to ring him again and texted him, but he didn't answer. She froze for a minute, not sure what to do next. Should she start checking for road accidents nearby online? Should she call the hospitals like they always do in the movies? Libbie was still going through all her options when her mobile's screen lit up. She opened Michael's text with a mix of anxiety and joy, as she now knew he was all right. Rage ran through her whole body and made her face red and hot. She threw the phone on the table, hitting the plate with a consequent noise that made the other patrons look at her. All the scrutinising eyes and Michael's untouched glass of Prosecco in front of her were a reminder he had actually dumped her and made the humiliation Libbie felt even more insufferable. She moved her chair away with excessive violence that only attracted more attention, got up, and gathered her belongings.

Outside in the parking lot, Libbie could not keep her nerves under control any longer. She screamed, removed her shoes, and threw them in the air. Once in the car, she turned the engine on and sped away, with no regard for the pedestrians in her way. Her eyes were full of rage, and even though she was looking at the road, she could not see it. She missed a turn and veered off the road. It took a moment before Libbie realised what had happened, then she checked for any injuries or damage to the car. Thankfully, both she and the car were both unharmed, but blood was dripping on her legs from her nose. This was all Michael's fault. She rang him again, and again without getting an answer. She was determined to let him know what he had done and that he would have to face the consequences of his actions. She sent him a text explaining she had an accident and he was to blame. With everything that had happened with McCabe and Bernadette, Michael had forgotten about his lunch date with Libbie. Well, if he was honest, he was never planning to go, and that was why he agreed to meet her at a distant restaurant in the first place. Michael never had the intention of showing up at the restaurant, and if things went according to plan, he would never have to worry about Libbie ever again. Unfortunately, he still didn't have a chance to talk to Bernadette, and now he had to find a plausible excuse to calm Libbie down. Michael stood in Libbie's living room, feeling he was becoming increasingly more trapped in a spider web of lies, but it was the only way to gain more time. Libbie would have to be patient a little longer, just enough for him to talk to his wife. When Michael left Libbie's flat, it was already late and he rang Bernadette to say he was on his way. After he hung up, Michael wondered if it was him or if he heard an actual surprise in Bernadette's voice. Then, he tried to remember the last time he did it. When was the last time they had lunch together? Or the last time he phoned home to say he was on his way, or to ask if there was something he had to get at the shops? He couldn't remember but for some reason tonight, it came spontaneously to him. Michael involuntary smiled for the feeling of normalcy he was experiencing; something he had lost for such a long time, without even realising it. He wanted to go home to his wife, talk to her, and spend some time with her. If only he didn't have to spoil their evening with his revelations. Suddenly, it was like his mistress became an annoying wife, and he wanted her out of his life. The woman who had intrigued him with that perfect body he had craved and enjoyed so many times before, was now not so appealing. She nearly disgusted him, while his long-time wife, the one he thought had nothing more to offer him, became the object of his desire instead.

40

"Hey, hon, I am leaving now. I'll be with you in ten, and I have cream eclairs."

"Sorry, but I don't feel well today." Jane only saw Bernadette's reply when she was already in the car, driving toward Green Hills. They had spoken yesterday morning and agreed on meeting today as Bernadette was supposed to help her out with her essay. Jane had won an online gardening course that required a final exam. Her text was short and sharp, unlike Bernadette's writing, which was usually very descriptive and adorned her texts with plenty of emojis. Jane decided to ring her friend to check on her but received no answer.

Jane and Bernadette had been friends since their childhood. They had always kept in touch even when life brought them to follow different paths. But ever since Bernadette moved back to the village, their friendship had gone back to the old days. Bernadette was an only child and Jane had two sisters who lived in England with whom she had not a very sisterly relationship. In the last 15 years, the two women became the closest thing to sisters for one another. Their kids were in school together, and their social and family lives progressed simultaneously, despite the fact their husbands were not the best of friends. Jane retired early from teaching after being diagnosed with breast cancer six years prior. During her illness, Bernadette was always there for her. She would bring her to chemotherapy whenever Tim couldn't, and helped in any way she could. Jane would feel forever grateful to her friend who pulled her through the worst. Tim had been brilliant, nobody denies it, but how could he have known what it felt like to only have one breast? Bernadette was there and had felt her pain with her. Ever since they were little, the difference in their personalities made their relationship that much stronger. They always complemented each other's personalities: the funny, exuberant Jane and the more conscious and private Bernadette. When Jane became sick, her bright side didn't fade on the surface, but Bernadette knew that sadness and depression ate away at her as much as cancer, and she fought it with her friend until they beat it together, making their friendship even stronger. Jane would always be grateful to Bernadette and loved her more than a sister but sometimes, she still felt there was a gap to fill between them, a hole going back over twenty-five years. No matter how much or how discretely she inquired, her friend never filled that gap. Why was Bernadette in such a hurry to marry Michael and have a child was a matter that they never discussed. She tried to make her wait at the time, but she was determined. One day she was gone, only to come back years later with a husband and a child. She, of course, respected her friend's will to keep some things to herself but at times, she felt there was much more to it than that and today, after that sharp text, the missed appointment and the missed call, she felt the same. Jane started to think about the last few weeks and had to admit that Bernadette had been quite elusive. She was nervous and out of reach. Even the night of the pub quiz she was distracted. Was she concerned, maybe? She had not paid much attention as she was busy herself with the course and everything but now, Jane started to think she maybe should have been more aware. Jane was already halfway there, so she decided to drive up to Bernadette's anyway. If she was genuinely sick, she would take on the role of the concerned friend that she was. But if it was just an excuse, then it was time for her friend to confide in her and tell her what was going on. Bernadette couldn't take her mind off what Michael had said about McCabe's visit at the clinic. She had forgotten about meeting Jane but now, she had far more important matters to take care of and right after Michael left, she headed off to Shane's. Jane would have had understood and as soon this mess was over, she would tell her everything.

"He's just fishing, Bernadette," Shane tried to reassure her.

"I know, but still, what if he uses Michael to corner us and start to spill the beans."

"Well, then we will think about it. Anyway, sooner or later, you will need to tell Michael and Samuel, right? Maybe it will be sooner."

Bernadette looked at him with panic and discouragement. She detached herself from him and walked away.

"Do you listen to yourself, Shane? Do you think it is that easy for me? You have nothing to lose, but I do. I have a family, a son and friends. I am lying to everybody I love, and have been lying even more since you've been back, or have you forgotten this?"

Bernadette was right, she had much more than Shane to lose if they exposed their story before they had time to talk to everyone involved, but still, Shane felt hurt by her words. What was she implying that he had forced her into this situation? Or was Bernadette changing her mind about him, about them? He knew he was asking a lot to her. Everything she had built in the last twenty-five years would be gone and destroyed. Shane looked at the woman in tears sitting on his couch and wondered if what they were doing was the right thing. It was right for him because he loved her more than anything in the world, since forever. But she was right, while Shane had nothing left but her and nothing to lose, she was putting her entire life at stake. He knew she loved him back with all her being but was he worth it? Did Shane have the right to ask her to sacrifice everything for him? Maybe if he loved her as much as he did, he should let her go—for her own sake. She would forget him again, and life would go on.

"You know what? You are right! Better you go."

Bernadette looked at him bewildered. What did he mean by go? Shane couldn't look at her, but he had to say it. He turned his back to Bernadette and leaned on the big sitting room window. "I said you better go, Bernie. Go home. We are done here."

"Shane..." Bernadette's voice was broken.

"Go home, Bernie, go away. What don't you understand? We are over. This is all too much for you, for me, for everybody." He paused for a second and then shouted at her once again to go, to leave his home. Bernadette ran home as fast as she could. Shane could not face seeing her go, so he stayed by the garden window until he heard the door close behind the woman only a few weeks ago he had sworn not to lose again.

He knew he was lying when he said that McCabe was only fishing. McCabe was no fool; he had no proof, but he would find it and get to the truth, he would not hesitate to drag everybody through the mud. Bernie didn't deserve this. Later, she would understand what he had done and why he had done it. Shane splattered some cold water on his face and scrolled the contacts on his phone until he found the one he was looking for. A couple of rings later, and a familiar voice answered at the other end of the line.

"It is me, Shane. We need to talk."

41

Jane pulled over in front of her best friend's house, got out of the car and rang the bell at the gate. She waited a few minutes, but when there was no answer, she rang again. Still, nobody answered. She wondered if Bernadette was just in bed resting, considering she was not well, allegedly not well, as more and more that brief, sharp text started to feel more like an excuse. What she could not figure out was why. Their friendship was solid and based on honesty. It was not exclusive and most of all, if one of the two didn't want to do something, they had never had to invent any excuses for one another. They had always been straightforward, and this was probably the recipe for their long friendship. Jane pictured two scenarios in her head: either she was becoming paranoid, or her friend was hiding something. The rational voice in her head was saying to leave. As Bernadette was unwell, or she simply had her reasons and she would give her best friend an explanation soon. Jane was notoriously not a rational person, nor a patient one and so she stayed. She had to know what was going on. If, there was something going on, of course. Jane tried to ring one more time before entering the gate code. While waiting for the gate to open, something on the side of the road caught Jane's attention. It was half-buried under a pile of leaves, but after she moved them aside, Jane immediately recognised what it was: the keyring she gave Bernadette the Christmas of the previous year. She would recognise it anywhere. It was stained with what looked like blood, and the keys had been removed before it was dumped. With the keyring in her hand, Jane jumped into her car and drove through the gate, which was now fully open. Bernadette's car was in the driveway, but the house was locked. She went around the side to see if the back door was opened, but it was closed too. The dogs inside were barking and frantically moving from one window to another. There was no sign of Bernadette and a wave of panic and concern started to rise inside Jane, and her heart began galloping. She was scrolling the recent calls on her mobile to call Tim when she saw the gate opening again. It was Bernadette. Her face was a mask of tears and smudged makeup, and her tights had holes in the knees and blood was dripping from them. Her hands were dirty from mud and scratched on the palms as she must have tripped on the road and tried to catch her fall with her hands. Jane ran toward her but neither of the two women said a word, until Bernadette handed Jane the house key to open the door she was shaking uncontrollably.

Once inside, Jane sat Bernadette on a kitchen chair and went to get some towels and Savlon to clean and disinfect the wounds. She put on the kettle and made some tea. Bernadette had eventually calmed down. She didn't question Jane's presence.

"I think it is time you gave me an explanation," Jane talked first, taking the keyring out of her pocket.

Bernadette instinctively brought one hand to her mouth, then started to talk. She told Jane everything, about the day of the finding and her affair with Shane. The words were flowing out her mouth like a flooded river. Jane took her friends hands in hers, she felt sorry that Bernadette had not confided in her, not because she didn't trust her but because she was protecting her.

"You need to talk to Shane. You belong together. No matter what he said. Trust me."

"You don't understand; he doesn't want to see me anymore. He thinks I don't want to talk to Michael. He thinks I am not sure I want to be with him, but I am! I never stopped loving him, but I need to protect Samuel first."

Jane looked at her friend and felt her pain. She handed her a napkin to blow her nose and wipe her tears.

"Samuel is a man now; he will understand, Bernadette," Jane genuinely thought that if the problem was how her adult son would react to his parents' divorce, this was nonsense.

"Michael will be furious; he will seek revenge and Samuel will be his weapon, and Shane will never forgive me. Maybe this is for the best." Bernadette felt exhausted and her look betrayed fear.

"Don't be ridiculous, Bernadette. Michael would never use his son. I am not particularly a fan of your cocky husband, but he would never do anything to hurt his son. And Shane will be more understanding than you think. After all, he waited for you for twenty-three years."

Bernadette abruptly stood up and started to shout at her friend. "What would you know? You don't know anything!

Samuel is not Michael's," she screamed, incapable of controlling her nerves and feeling furious for the mess she had put herself and everybody she loved, in.

This time, it was Jane to cover her mouth in bewilderment.

"Yes, I am a terrible person. I lied to everybody all these years, even to you," Bernadette regained some lucidity.

She had already regretted what she had just said, but it was too late. If the roles were reversed, she would have been furious with Jane to have mistrusted her for so long, and she expected Jane to be the same. Jane was speechless. She looked at her best friend without recognising the woman that was standing in front of her. Bernadette sat back down and told her everything that happened after Shane left.

She told Jane how she had discovered she was pregnant straight after Shane left, and by the time he contacted her again, she had met Michael who had offered to marry her and raise Samuel as though he was his son. Bernadette was not shouting anymore. She had no energy left. When she had finished talking, she felt so much lighter but also empty and ashamed for what she had done. She didn't have the courage to look Jane in the eye because she was not sure what she would see.

Hate, disgust, pity, compassion. Jane was feeling all these emotions at once. She understood why Bernadette did what she did and felt terrible for her as nobody of such a young age should ever go through what she went through. She could appreciate that she got caught up in her web of lies, but she could not forgive her for not having trusted her enough to tell her the truth over the years.

"I'm sorry, Bernadette. I really am. For what you have gone through and for what you are going through now, and I swear my lips are sealed, but I can't understand how you could have kept lying to me for all these years. You had plenty of chances to tell me the truth. After all, we went through so much together. I thought I deserved more consideration from you, of all people," Jane spoke calmly, trying to keep her voice steady and the tears away from her eyes. She grabbed her purse and left.

42

Michael's explanations over the phone didn't calm Libbie down. He had to talk to her in person. When Michael arrived at her flat, she was in an awful state. There was blood on her face, probably from her bleeding nose, but she was all right—at least physically.

The "accident", if it really ever happened, had left her uninjured. Michael felt nothing but contempt for the woman in front of him but he had to play along, so he consoled her and held her until she eventually calmed down. After Michael left, Libbie took her dress off and threw it out it as it was no longer the symbol of a new start but just a reminder of how it had been ruined. She removed her drenched tights and went to the bathroom to wash her face. She looked horrible. She had cried so much that her eyes were red and puffy and still full of hate. She could see her rage reflected in the mirror; just now her anger was not for Michael anymore but for Bernadette instead. She was the only obstacle to her new glamorous life and no matter how hard Michael was trying, his wife was determined not to let him go. However, Libbie would never allow her to keep him from her. She removed the leftover traces of makeup and started to run a hot bath. Immersed in the water, she eventually felt her body relax, and her mind gradually let the anger go to make space for some rationality. She had already fallen so many times in her short life but this time, falling was not an option, and neither was giving Michael more time. She could not trust him to solve anything. Libbie knew he wanted to be with her but like most men, he was weak. It was time for Libbie to take matters in her own hands and this time; she was not going to make the same mistake again. She had made the mistake of underestimating Bernadette once, but she won't do it again. That insignificant little creature was more dangerous than she thought and she was ready to use all the cards she had up her sleeve to keep her husband.

"A pity you don't know who you are fighting against, darling," Libbie said to her reflected image, imagining she was speaking to her rival. She changed into some yoga pants and a T-shirt poured herself some wine and curled up on the sofa thinking at how easy it would be to make Bernadette disappear, the same way Paul did.

43

"…And that is all," Shane leaned back in his chair, feeling like he had removed the heaviest of the weights from his shoulders. Billy believed him, but he still had not said a word. At the little desk under the window, Annette had stopped typing when Shane had stopped talking, and she was now staring at her boss for further instructions. Except, Billy had no idea of what to do. Shane's words were as truthful as they were incriminating. He regretted Annette had to stay in the room and type Shane's confession, but at the same time, he knew he had no choice. He could not risk his career for Shane, but he needed a private word with him.

"Annette, you can go now. Print Mr Flynn's deposition and wait outside."

"But, chief..." Annette tried to protest, but Billy shushed her brusquely with his hand. The young Gardaí left and shut the door noisily behind her.

"What the fuck, Shane?" Billy got up and went to the cabinet on the other side of the room. He unlocked the first drawer and took out two glasses and a bottle of Bushmill. Shane was still silent and only had a sip of his drink, while Billy already drained his glass in one shot.

"You do whatever you have to do, Billy. I am not asking for any favouritism here. I know I should have told you everything since the beginning and I know how bad I look now, but there is nothing I can do to change things now. The only thing I ask you is to leave Bernie out of it. She has nothing to do with anything. She doesn't deserve her name on everybody's mouth, and have her life destroyed along with her husband's and son's."

"Well, it is a bit late now to think of Samuel and Michael, isn't it?" Billy could not help but snap. He believed Shane and was genuinely sorry for him and Bernadette. He also admired the man that was willing to take full responsibility just to protect the woman he loved, but he was a man of law, and even if he wanted to ignore Bernadette's involvement and the few details of the whole story, Annette typed the complete deposition and heard every single word that Shane spoke.

"You know I can't do that, Shane. I can't ignore half of your deposition, and I can't ask Annette to be an accomplice in a cover-up."

"But you believe me, right? You believe we have nothing to do with Paul's death?"

As a human being, Billy understood that the self-preservation mechanism had brought Shane to hide the truth, and his will to protect Bernadette. Billy himself would have probably done the same to protect Martha, but he could not let his feelings and personal beliefs interfere with his investigation. That said, he also wanted to limit the damage for everybody involved. Billy needed a bit more time to find a solution and a way.

"Bloody hell, Shane, I wished you had never come to talk to me. Bad enough you and Bernadette buried yourselves in deep shit, but you dragged Annette and me into it too."

"I am sorry, Billy, I am." Shane's face was the face of a scared child who had no idea how to get out of trouble without letting his parents know he got into trouble in the first place.

The chief poured two more glasses of whiskey and this time; both men drank them straight and in one shot.

"Now, listen to me, Shane. You go home and do not talk to anybody about our conversation. Give me a day or two, ok?"

"Ok." Shane's tone was full of gratitude and admiration. "And what about Bernie?" Shane knew he was pushing it now, but he had to ask.

"I will need to call her to the station, Shane, and see what she has to say, but we might be able to keep it quiet and discrete."

How, when, why... Shane wanted to ask what would happen to her, to him, to them but he knew better than to ask any further questions. The man had already agreed to expose himself far too much than he had intended, and Shane would never forget it.

"Do you want to get drunk or do you want to tell me what the fuck is going on, chief?"

George Polinsky was standing by the door of the sergeant's office. Billy nearly fell from his chair when he saw him.

"Annette filled me in and showed me the deposition while you were having your little private chat with one of your primary suspects."

"It is not as simple as it looks, George. Besides, last time I checked, it was still my investigation."

"And still is, Billy, for now. Listen, I'm not here to get you into trouble, but you need to fill me in properly. I told you from the upper floors they are now starting to ask for closure. I need to know what is going on and which direction you are going. I am not here to question your professionalism, but I think I deserve some trust and honesty."

George Polinsky was right. After Billy told him everything, he knew Polinsky agreed about the extraneousness of Shane and Bernadette to the murder, but he suggested he bring her down to the station and question her, regardless. She might have seen something useful for the investigation that afternoon, without even realising it. In the meantime, he would try to keep the superintendent at bay for as long as he could.

"I can't promise you anything, Billy. I'll do my best to get you more time but the fact remains, you have no leads and I won't be able to justify it forever."

"You won't have to." Billy's words sounded convincing, but both men knew there was nothing to support them yet. The front door closed and Annette knocked and slowly and shyly opened Billy's office door. He was standing by the window with a glass in his hand.

"I am sorry, boss. I didn't want to tell him but he asked who you were with and I had to." Annette's upset voice made him feel sorry for her, and for the way he treated her before and for the fact that she was apologising for doing nothing but her job. She was not the one who had to apologise; he was.

44

Billy McCabe was snoring on the couch when a noise came from the hall and woke him up. It was far too early for Martha to be home from her monthly book club meeting. The sergeant jumped to his feet and reached for his gun on his belt, forgetting he had already secured it in the safe. That was a habit his father passed on. When he got back from the station, Billy McCabe Sr. used to remove his shoes and jacket in the hall first, then he would put away the gun in a locked drawer at his desk. Trying to make the least noise possible, Billy grabbed the fireplace poker and went straight for the possible intruder. He opened the hall's door and switched on the light, branding the poker in the air. He was ready to strike when a scream from a familiar voice made him freeze. "Jeez, Billy. Are you out of your mind? You could have killed me with that thing." Martha leaned against the wall to regain her breath.

"Honey, I am sorry, I thought it was someone trying to break in," Billy dumped the club on the floor and hugged his wife.

"But what are you doing home so early?"

"Well, it turned out that it was only Emily and me and Jane didn't show up, and Bernadette sent a text saying she was not feeling well, so there was no point in discussing anything, I guess. We had a drink, then decided to reschedule."

"Well, not too bad then, I can have you all for myself," Billy winked at his wife with a big smile on his face. She knew what he had in mind.

"Well, chief, how can I resist a man of the law?" Martha kissed her husband on the lips and started to lead the way upstairs. Halfway up the stairs, Billy's mobile began to vibrate in his pocket. Martha could hear the noise. Billy decided to ignore the call except the phone didn't stop ringing. Whoever it was, they were not giving up. Martha and Billy had reached their bedroom, and the sergeant had removed his trousers. The noise of the vibrating phone on the floor was impossible to ignore.

"You might want to see what they want, Billy," Martha said. She was used to having her plans ruined because of a work call.

"What is it?" Billy barked into the phone.

"Fuck, ok I will be there in ten."

"Billy, is everything ok?" Martha knew that if something happened, he couldn't share too many details, only some.

"There has been shooting up in Green Hills. I have to go, love, sorry."

The road was pitch dark, but a car from the other town was already there, with the flashing lights still on. A small crowd of curious neighbours came out of the nearby houses. Annette arrived shortly after him. He had called her on his way over.

"Thank you, guys. I will take it from here. Who had phoned the 999?" The two uniform officers, probably out in patrol from Barrystown, pointed to an elderly man on the side of the road. Billy went straight to him, trying to understand what happened.

"I can't say much, chief. I was walking the dog when I heard a shot and a car losing control as it veered off the road and into that tree, see," the man showed him precisely where he was standing when it happened, "if that tree was not there, it could have hit Robbie or me, you know?"

"So, there was someone else with you?" Billy asked in the hope that someone with better sight and memory could provide details on what happened too.

"Yes, I just told you, my dog, Robbie, we were out for his evening wee."

"Yes, right," Billy disappointedly replied.

"And have you seen the shooter or if there was someone else on the road?"

"No, chief, as I said, my sight is not the best in the dark." Billy could not help but wonder if it was any better in the daylight, but this witness was all he had, "Did you hear some noise or see some unfamiliar car parked around the area?"

"No, nothing, it was like any other evening. But, now that you mention it, I heard some noise in the bushes, straight after the car was hit, but I didn't pay attention because animals are always wandering around in the fields at night, and I was already in shock by then."

"Of course, thank you. Anyway, you have been of great help, Mr... ?" Billy knew the man from the church, but he never knew his name.

"O'Leary, Frank O'Leary. Can I go home now? My wife will be worried sick about Robbie and me, as we are never out for more than 20 minutes at this hour."

"Of course, Mr O'Leary, but we will need to talk again, and you will have to come to the station to sign your deposition. In the meanwhile, if you can think of anything that could be of any help, please ring me, even if it is something insignificant." The chief gave Mr O'Leary his number and joined Annette, who was by the car with the forensic circus already at work.

"So, chief, it looks like your little village is getting very active lately or should I say, deadly active?"

Billy was in no mood for Philips' jokes and sarcasm and went to Dr Campion. The coroner was bent above the body inside the car.

"Male, middle age, one shot penetrated the front window and hit him in the forehead, causing him to lose control of the car. I can't say if it was the shot for the bang on the steering wheel that caused his death, but he had his wallet with him," she said, passing it to Annette who immediately checked inside.

"Oh, shit, boss, you better see this."

45

Only Annette and Billy were left at the scene.

They were waiting for the tow truck to take the car away when a big SUV pulled over in front of them and an alarmed Shane Flynn got out.

"What the fuck happened? That is Bernie's car. Is she ok? Where is she?" Shane Flynn had just returned from a business meeting in Dublin and saw the familiar half-destroyed car on the side of the road. His eyes were coming out of their sockets, and he was shaking. He could only think of what he said to her the previous day and now she might have gone forever. How could he live with that?

"Calm down, Shane. Bernadette must be fine. She was not in the car at the time of the accident."

"What? Who was in there? What happened?"

"Shane, look at me," Billy's tone was calm but authoritative, "I need you to go home and stay there. We can't tell you more than this at the moment, but I promise Bernadette was not involved in the accident."

"But that is her car, I don't understand… who was in it?"

"For fuck's sake, Shane. Go home. I have no time for you now." Billy was losing his patience.

The situation was complicated enough, last thing he needed was having Shane Flynn around.

"Annette, bring Mrs Greaney a glass of water, would you?" Annette went to the kitchen, while Billy tried to calm a frantic Bernadette down.

Michael's death made it much more complicated for the sergeant to talk to her about the other murder, and the last thing he wanted to do was to question her about her affair with Shane and her possible involvement in Paul's murder while telling her that her own husband had just been murdered himself. Bernadette took the water with extreme gratitude. Her throat was dry and her head blurry. She felt tipsy without drinking.

"I don't understand, who could have possibly wanted to kill Michael?"

A heavy silence descended on the room.

"Wait a minute, Billy, are you thinking I have something to do with it?"

"I don't know, Bernadette. You tell me. There is a lot you haven't told me, and as much as I don't want to believe you have anything to do with your husband's death or Paul's, I have to ask: where were you tonight?"

Bernadette's face contorted into a grin of disbelief for everything that was happening to her.

"I was home alone."

"Were you sick?"

"No. Just home, like any other evening," her tone was not upset or angry but defeated. She looked guilty and she knew it.

"Listen, Bernadette, I am sorry about all this and despite what you might think I am not enjoying myself here, putting you on the spot and under scrutiny. But I have to do my job."

Bernadette looked a Billy with tearful eyes, that told him she had no grudge against him.

"I say you have gone through enough tonight but tomorrow you will have to come down to the station for some questioning and a signed deposition."

"Ok, thank you, Billy. I mean it."

Bernadette spontaneously hugged the big man in front of her and when realising what she had just done, she detached herself from him immediately. An embarrassed Sergeant McCabe cleared his throat, "It might be better for you not to stay alone tonight. Is there someone we can call? Jane, maybe?"

Hearing Jane's name hurt Bernadette like a stab. Jane was her rock and the first person she would have called, if she was still talking to her.

"No, I don't think Jane would come. Not as things are now."

Billy was surprised as even from what Martha always said, the two women were inseparable.

"We had a fight the other day and she hasn't spoken to me since. That is why I didn't want to go to the book club meeting. I just pretended to be unwell so I wouldn't have to see her," Bernadette added, as she felt Billy deserved some explanations.

"What about your son?"

Bernadette froze. How could she have forgotten about Samuel? She had to call him. She had to tell him... everything.

"I don't even know what time it is in Boston now."

"If you want, we can ring him," Billy offered and went on, "but, if it was me and my father died, I would want to receive that phone call straight away from my mother, no matter the time of the day or night."

"Yes, you're right."

After she had escorted Annette and Billy to the door, Bernadette blew her nose with some kitchen paper, dried her tears and tried to compose herself, if only for the benefit of her son.

46

"So, what do you think, chief?"

"I don't know, Annette. It is just a big mess, and I am expecting the superintendent to call any minute now. Not to mention, we still have no clue who killed Paul, but as God is my witness, I am sure the two crimes are in some way connected."

"Sir, I couldn't sleep last night, and so I prepared this." Annette unfolded a big sheet of paper and hung it on the board in Billy's office. Billy looked at it with scepticism.

"I know what you are thinking, sir, that we are not on an episode of *Criminal Minds* but putting everything we know in a scheme can help us connect the dots."

Billy went closer to the board and stared at the sheet.

Annette took a step back; she knew he was thinking of something.

"Give me that marker, would you?" Pleased and proud that her idea was working, Annette passed the red pen to her boss and watched him crossing and connecting the main characters and places of their investigation.

"Any word from Dr Campion?"

"No, not yet, sir."

"Give her a call and see if she can speed it up for us."

Half an hour later, the report from the coroner arrived on Billy's desk and after reading it, he called his deputy in:

"Have a look and tell me what you think."

"It is the same gun that was used to kill Paul."

"Exactly. A bit too much of a coincidence, isn't it?" Billy's faith in Bernadette and Shane been estranged to the events was gradually fading.

"And if we think who had a motive and an opportunity to kill them both, we need to go back to the two reconciled lovers," Annette concluded.

"Unfortunately, Annette, and it has always been right there in front of me. I just refused to see it, and I let them fool me."

"Don't beat yourself up, chief. I must confess, I was totally convinced of their innocence too, by the end. Besides, they have an alibi for Paul's murder. It might not be the best, and they are each other's alibi, but still, we can't prove anything."

"I know, and in fact, we will question them only for Dr Greany's death. We can hold them for 48 hours and hopefully it will be enough to break them. We will need to question Bernadette first as she is the one who gets all the advantages from her husband's death. She will be free and rich. Plus, she has no real alibi for that night. On the contrary, she already gave two versions of her whereabouts of the evening. Bernadette told the book club she was sick, but she told me she actually wasn't. She said she simply didn't want to go to see Jane, who was not there either. In the end, Bernadette had no real reason to find an excuse to not go to the meeting."

"Unless she had something to do," Annette finished her boss'sentence.

"Exactly."

The gate of the Greaney's residence was opened, and Billy drove straight through. He knocked on the door and to his surprise, Shane opened the door. The two men looked at each other in silence for a few seconds, then before the sergeant could ask anything, Shane said, "I just came to see how she was. I couldn't stay at home doing nothing. I am sure you understand. She is a mess. First me and my damn mouth, then Michael."

"Of course." Billy was sharp and brief in his reply. He didn't want to engage in conversation. He was there to perform his duty, and he couldn't afford to let himself be conditioned once again. Either these two were innocent and he was fishing in the wrong pool, or they were among the best liars he had ever met.

"Billy…" Bernadette walked toward the sergeant and was about to greet him when Billy started reciting the words she heard so many times in the movies but had never dreamed of hearing them uttered to her.

"Bernadette Greaney, you are under arrest for the murder of your husband, Michael Greaney. You have the right…" Billy was like an old vinyl, playing his refrain regardless of the objections coming from the other two parties. Billy opened the car door and gently helped a handcuffed Bernadette in.

"Wait!" Shane was standing behind Billy. "I did it. I killed Michael."

Bernadette's mouth opened in disbelief.

"Oh, really?" the sergeant's voice was a mock.

"Yes, I just faked my meeting in Dublin. I waited for everybody to leave the scene, then I pretended to have just arrived to give myself an alibi."

Billy turned toward Shane. "And what have you done with the rifle?"

"I ditched it, and I was planning to report it stolen today."

Billy slammed the car door and got into the driver's seat. He closed the door and turned the window down, while Shane was still there, waiting. "Just a pity the weapon that shot Michael's car was a handgun. Now, do yourself and your lady a favour and stop filling me with bullshit. You already have a pending account for obstruction of justice, let's not make it two or worse."

Billy drove away, leaving Shane powerless, his hands in his head. Now what?

47

The latest news of Dr Michael Greaney's death and his wife's arrest were already circulating in the village. The villagers had split in two, with one side believing that such a sweet woman like Bernadette could never do something like that, while the other found the other side much more entertaining—a gory love triangle ending in the murder of the inconvenient husband. Billy had failed to avoid any leaks but at least he had managed not to leak the name of the alleged "other man". Martha was sitting opposite him at the dinner table with a worryingly angry expression. "Seriously, you had to take her into the station handcuffed, so that everybody could see?" Billy lowered his eyes and said nothing; he knew his wife had to rant. "I was in Maude's this afternoon, and that bunch of angry chickens were talking of nothing else."

Billy had to use all his willpower not to laugh at his wife's remark. He knew who she was referring to—a group of women who preferred to focus their energy on other people's lives rather than living their own. It had always made him laugh the way she called them "the angry chickens", a definition that surely a man was not allowed to use when referring to women, but it was ok if women themselves used it.

"And what about Samuel? Poor boy, his father is dead, and his mother is in jail for his murder."

When Martha got up to grab one of her favourite chocolates, her husband could finally take a breath of relief as that was the sign that her scene was over and she was starting to metabolise the whole situation. She sat back at the table and greedily unwrapped the chocolate, then stuffed it into her small mouth. Her gaze was back on Billy now, like she was expecting an explanation.

"Listen, Martha. I know you two are friends and you like her very much, and so do I."

Martha tipped her head and an incredulous expression appeared on her face.

"I really do and deep down, I am still hoping she will be innocent, but I have to do my job. I have to look at the facts, and I know you understand."

Martha's eyes filled again with her usual sweetness and the tenderness she usually reserved for her husband.

"I know, love, it's just that his whole thing is like a plot of a very bad movie. I can't believe Bernadette could have done something like that."

"Frankly, neither can I, but some people are good at hiding their dark side and when we like them, we sometimes refuse to see the truth."

Martha fell silent and soon Billy understood that it was not a sign of implicit consent. Something was bothering her.

"Martha? Is there something you know and want to tell me?"

After all the years together, Billy knew when his wife had something on her mind.

"No, really, just..." Martha was nervously playing with the hem of the tablecloth, and without looking at her husband, she went on talking, "... there were rumours in the village about Michael having indiscretions and..." Billy was getting slightly upset now, as when he asked Martha before, she said nothing.

"Martha, what do you know?"

"I know nothing for sure, Billy, that is why I never bothered to tell you. They are just stupid village rumours and are probably invented by those mean women."

"Well, you should have let me decide if it was important or not," Billy said, raising his voice. When Martha had finished telling him what they were saying in the village, he had to agree that there was nothing helpful in those rumours. They sounded generated more from jealousy than real facts. In fairness, Michael Greaney was the perfect advertisement of men in their mid-life crises: his fitness obsession, flashy car, stylish clothes and, why perhaps some indiscretion here and there. It was entirely credible that his wife had some distraction too: the lonely and neglected wife who finally reunited with her first love. Martha was right, it was more material for a Harmony book than a murder case but still, at the bottom of every rumour, there is always something real. The problem was that he had no facts, and the facts he did have were against Bernadette.

48

Jane was facing the window overlooking their back garden, staring into the space in front of her. After her argument with Bernadette, she had not contacted her friend, not even after Michael was killed. She had not said anything to Tim, but he was no fool, and she knew he had noticed how upset she was in the last few days. Tim didn't ask, and she appreciated it because she didn't really know what to say to him. Jane was still hurt by the lies she had been told all these years, but at the same time, she couldn't hate the woman who was more than a sister to her, and she knew that with the last events, she should have put aside her rancour and offered her help. However, she had not had the courage to do it yet. She had been so harsh on Bernadette the last time they spoke that she even doubted she would still want her by her side. The doorbell rang, but she didn't bother with it and let Tim open the door. Jane could hear him talking to someone, then the door closed but the voices were still audible. Whoever had rung the door was now inside the house. After a few minutes, Tim showed up in the kitchen where Jane was still staring outside the window.

"Jane, it's Sam. You better come in the sitting room."

"I don't feel like talking to him. I don't know what to say. I don't even know if his mother wants me to talk to him, or her anymore." Jane didn't turn but Tim understood from her voice that she was on the verge of crying and gently took his wife by her shoulders and made her face him. Tears were running down her pale face.

"Listen to me, Jane, I don't know what happened between you and Bernadette but in the other room, there is a very scared boy who just lost his father, and he might lose his mother too."

Jane's eyes suddenly lit up as she received an electric wave.

"What are you talking about?"

"He arrived this morning and went straight home from the airport, but the police wouldn't let him in. They are searching the house now, and they took Bernadette in custody with the charge of having killed Michael." It took a few seconds for Jane to recover from the shock of what she just heard. She wiped the tears away from her face, straightened her shoulders and without saying a word, went to the sitting room. Sam was sitting on the sofa like a wounded little bird who had fallen from the nest. Jane sat beside him and embraced him in a warm tight hug.

"What is going on, Auntie Jane? I don't understand. They say my mum killed dad, and they wouldn't even let me see her. I am sorry, but I didn't know what else to do." The young man broke down in a flood of tears.

"It is ok, darling, let it out," Jane said, patting his back in comfort.

"I'll make you tea, and we will see what we can do. But one thing I can tell you already, your mother would never do such a thing." Jane got up and with a stroke of the head, told Tim, who was standing by the door, to follow her into the kitchen.

"Did you know about this?" She looked inquisitively at her husband.

"No, it must have happened this morning, and since I haven't gone to the office yet, I had no way of hearing about it. I didn't even check the news yet."

"Ok, we need to go to the station and see what is going on and you, Tim, have to go as her lawyer."

"I am a solicitor, Jane. I am not a criminal lawyer. We need to call someone else."

"I know that, but at least you know the law, and you will understand what they are saying and doing. You can make sure they are acting properly, following the rules and aren't abusing their power. In the meanwhile, we will call someone else. We can call, what's his name, the guy you used to sail with..."

"Gerry, yes, that is a good idea. I will ring him straight away and ask him to come down as soon as he can. Besides, he owes me a couple of favours."

Tim was about to leave the room, then stopped and went back to his wife, "I am proud of you. Whatever might have happened between the two of you, this is bigger. You are doing the right thing." Jane looked up at him and smiled tenderly, they kissed, and he went off to make the phone call, while Jane went back to Sam.

"Ok. Gerry will come as soon as he can, but it might be not before tonight or tomorrow morning because he is out of town. But he instructed me about what to do as her initial legal representative. I am just getting my briefcase, and I'll go to the station. You can come as well, just be prepared not to see her, but you might want to inquire about when she can go back home," Tim said, looking at Sam who had grabbed his coat and was ready to go.

"I'll come too." Jane had no intention of staying behind and ran after the two men.

"Ok then, now it is up to you, Sam, whether you want to go back home or if you would rather stay with us today and tonight."

"Auntie Jane, uncle Tim, do you mind if I stay with you? At least until mum comes home?"

"Of course," the couple said in unison, but Jane saw an alarming glimpse of concern in Tim's face when Sam mentioned his mother's return home. None of them spoke during the drive back home. Jane opened the door making her best not to show Sam how afraid she was for his mother.

"Come with me, darling; the guest room is not ready, but Laura's room has fresh linens. I always keep her bed ready in case she decides to stop by. You never know with her, as I am sure you remember." Jane attempted a laugh and Sam, appreciating her will to try to ease his pain, faked a laugh back. "Yes, you never really know what is going on in that daughter of yours' head, do you?" Laura was a couple of years younger than Sam and always had a crush on him. She was like dynamite in a pocket but one of the cleverest human beings he had never known, as proved by the fact that after she had finished college over a year in advance, she was immediately hired by an international chemical company in Oslo.

"Ok, I'll let you get comfortable and have a rest now. You must be exhausted." Jane gave Sam a loving pat on his arm and left the room, closing the door behind her.

Tim was waiting for her in the kitchen, even if she had said nothing, he knew she had questions.

"Ok, between you and me, how bad is the situation? Honestly?"

"At the moment, they have nothing concrete against her but as the good old Poirot used to say: one coincidence is just a coincidence, two coincidences are a clue, three coincidences are proof, and there are lots of coincidences there. Bernadette has had quite the lively life recently. What do you know about it, Jane? Is it because of this that the two of you argued?" Jane sat down and started to tell her husband everything Bernadette revealed to her

"Oh, boy!" Tim couldn't believe what he had just heard. It was something he thought that only happened in the movies and quite frankly if what his wife just revealed to him became public, it could only aggravate Bernadette's position as it could be seen as she had even more motive.

"And do you know who else knows about the whole story, the truth about the child I mean?"

"I have no idea, Tim. I don't think anybody knows. Shane for sure doesn't, and neither does Sam, of course. Aside from us, the only two people to know the truth were Bernadette and Michael."

"As I feared, and now Michael is dead... you know what it means, right?"

"You wouldn't think she killed him to keep her secret safe, do you? I don't even know she wants to keep the secret anymore." Jane was horrified that Tim could even only consider such an allegation.

"I want to believe she is estranged to Michael's death as much as you do, Jane, but we need to look at things rationally. Hiding our heads in the sand will do no good—to anyone. I need to talk to her again. I need to know the facts straight from her mouth, and so will Gerry."

"Oh, I don't know, Tim. I don't think it is up to us whether she wants to tell or not. Maybe we should wait and see." Jane didn't want to betray her friend. Telling Bernadette's secret to Tim was one thing—he was her husband— but saying it to a stranger, whether it was the lawyer or not, was an utterly different thing.

"And think about Sam, what if something reaches his ears? Or Shane's? It could potentially be the end of any relationship Bernadette has with either of them."

"It is because I am thinking about Sam that I am saying this, Jane. No truth will be worse than seeing his mother in jail for his father's murder. And our only chance to avoid this is to get to the bottom of this bloody mess."

49

Libbie went home and opened a bottle of wine to celebrate her future as Mrs Greaney, and for definite this time. She had waited in the dark until she saw the body carried away in a black bag. Bernadette was not an obstacle to her life with Michael anymore. Of course, in the beginning, they might have to keep a low profile as he is now a newly widowed man, but they will eventually be free to live their love. And Samuel, he will love her. She is young enough to know what young people of his age like and did, and she was sure to get into her future stepson's sympathies pretty easily. He might resist her at the beginning, but she will win him over in the end. The following morning, her head was still heavy from the bottle of wine she had drunk the night before. She prepared a strong black coffee, then called Michael. He didn't answer; he was probably busy with the police. Libbie's new beginning was starting today. She went through her wardrobe and began to select the most appropriate outfits for her new life, and she did the same with her shoes. She threw herself into the shower and got dressed, accordingly with her new status. Never mind anybody else, they would soon find out. She went out for breakfast and had a walk, as the weather was finally dry and sunny, after a few days of rain. She was walking on the strand when she tried to ring Michael again, and this time, someone picked up just after a couple of rings. It was a woman's voice that Libbie had not recognised. She instinctively hung up and dialled the number again with the false hope to have got it wrong the first time. Libbie stopped and remained silent, while the woman's voice introduced herself as a tech operator with the national forensic department and asked who it was. Libbie didn't know what to think. Why does some forensic person have Michael's phone? Where was he? Maybe something happened to him? She went to the local newspaper Facebook page to read the latest local news: *Another murder in Seacross. The well-known Dr Greaney was the victim of a fatal car accident last night. Unconfirmed sources close to the local Garda station said that the village dentist lost control of his car after a gunshot hit the front window of the vehicle and died from the impact...*

Libbie didn't need to keep reading the whole article. She started to scream at full voice. People on the street were looking at her, but she couldn't care less. What else did she have to lose now? She started to run, and she ran until she got home.

"What have I done?" she screamed repeatedly. Like a broken disc, Libbie kept shouting that very same question, while throwing everything she could put her hands on around the flat. She went to her bedroom and started to rip apart all her clothes and break all the heels off her shoes until her hands hurt. Eventually, she sat on the bed, exhausted. How could this have happened? She saw Bernadette's car leaving the house. It was dark because the gate lamp was not working, but it was her car! And Michael never drove it. He hated that old thing, so why was he even in it? More rage and more exhaustion possessed her. She had lost everything, and forever this time. This time, there was no coming back.

50

After Tim went through everything with Bernadette again, something got his attention.

"So, Michael was not driving his car that night?"

"No, I told you. He took mine because the keys were by the door. He had left his in his blazer upstairs. He just had to go to Maude's to get some milk."

"Ok, was it normal for him to use your car? And run errands like that?"

"No. He hated driving my car. He only took it because it was faster than going upstairs to get his keys. Besides, he only had to drive down to the village. But why, what does this have to do with what happened?"

"Right. Listen to me carefully now, Bernadette. It is possible that the target was you and not him?" If the situation was not so dramatic, Bernadette would have had a laugh at Tim's words.

"Me? Who would want to kill me?"

Tim didn't have an answer to her question, but everything pointed at it and this was the best lead to prove his friend's innocence.

"Well, who would have wanted to kill your husband?"

Tim had a point; Bernadette could see it.

"I want you to think back over the last few months or weeks. Did anything out of the ordinary happen? How was Michael?"

With slight embarrassment, Bernadette started to reveal the poverty of her marriage.

"We were moving apart, Tim. I thought it was because of me but now, I am not so sure. What are you implying? What do you know?"

"I don't know anything, Bernadette. I am just trying to find some logic to what happened. How was he?"

"Everything was normal, Tim, the same old life. He was going to work and coming home. Nothing really out of the ordinary, except for that golf trip."

"What golf trip?" If there was a golf trip, Tim should have known about it.

"You know, the one with the old guys, down in the Southside. Michael said you couldn't go, but I don't remember why."

"There was no golf trip, Bernadette."

"What do you mean there was no golf trip?"

"Exactly what I said. There was no golf trip in the Southside."

"Then, where did he go for the entire weekend?"

Bernadette's face had aged ten years in a day. Tim couldn't say if she was hurt by her husband's lies, but he could certainly say she was exhausted and defeated. He, on the other hand, started to see some way of escape because even though he was not a criminal lawyer, he knew how to connect the dots. Something that apparently the chief still needed practice on.

Michael's reputation, with a fake golf trip and what he saw the night of the quiz pub when he was going into the gents, was enough for him to get the sergeant's attention.

"Ok, I need to talk to Billy now. You stay put and don't say anything to anybody."

"Tim, wait, what is going on?" Bernadette's words were left pending in the air.

"Annette, where is the chief?"

"He will be here any minute."

"Call him. Tell him to come as soon as he can."

"No offence, sir, but I do not take orders from you."

"Annette, I said call him, right now, Goddamn it." Tim himself was surprised by his outburst and judging from the young guard's face, she was too. But before any of them could say or do anything, Billy McCabe entered the station.

"What's going on here?"

Tim explained his theory to Billy and even if it was all circumstantial, it supported what Martha told him and his idea of Bernadette being incapable of hurting a fly.

"Annette, call Philips and see if they have the phone records for Dr Greaney's mobile." Billy said, then turned toward Tim, "You understand that I can't ask for a warrant without something in my hands, right? That means it might require a bit of time." Tim didn't care about time; he just cared about proving Bernadette innocent.

"Sir, Philips want to talk to you."

"Right, pass me the phone."

"Sergeant McCabe, ~~what~~ do you think that your little countryside murders are the only cases we have?" Billy covered the phone speaker with his big hand and muttered something. He had no time for Philips's sarcasm right now, and thankfully, Philips went back to talking on the other end of the line. "Anyway..." Philips liked to keep his audience in suspense. "...because we are incredibly efficient, even if we don't have the phone records yet, I can tell you that my colleague here answered two phone calls on the deceased's mobile this morning. It came from the same number listed on his most frequently called list. We did a little checking, and the number belongs to the widow of your first murder victim." Billy didn't answer and hung up in a hurry. He had what he needed for that search warrant. After a few seconds, the phone rang again.

"You have to work on your manners, McCabe."

"Sorry, Philips. Did I forget to thank you for doing your job?" Billy snapped. He had no time for Philips' prima donna tantrums.

"As you did, Billy boy. And if you had let me finish, you would have heard me say that the same gun used to kill Paul was also used to kill Michael, and the fingerprints on the bullets match. The same hand killed both men."

"Thank you, Philips, I owe you a pint." Never in his life had Billy felt sympathy for Philips, but he had just given him the most crucial pieces of information to solve two cases at once.

"Annette, we need an extra urgent search warrant for the flat of Libbie Mulligan. Send it to my mobile as soon as you get it."

"I don't understand, sir; what does Paul's widow have to do with this..?"

"Annette, do what I asked, NOW."

McCabe left the station followed by a grateful Tim. They parked right outside the main entrance of the apartment block. They tried the bell but there was no answer, so they had to ask a neighbour to open the main entrance door. Libbie's flat was on the third floor. The lift was out of service and Tim and Billy had to take the stairs. At the second floor, they had to stop and take a breath and when they were ready to climb the last ramp, a door opened and an elderly lady stepped out onto the landing.

"Are you here for Mrs Mulligan?"

"Maybe." Billy didn't want to disclose the reason for their presence or feed neighbourhood gossips.

"She lives right above me, and earlier, it sounded like the third world war was happening up there. I was about to go up to her and complain, but the noise suddenly stopped."

"Ok, thank you. Now you go back inside, and we will go and check."

The apartment's door was, fortunately, not locked, and Billy managed to open it with his credit card. Tim was impressed as the only time he ever tried to do that, he failed, and he and Jane had to call the locksmith and replace the entire lock. The lady downstairs was right; it was like a bomb had blown up in there. The entire flat was destroyed.

"You stay here, "Billy ordered Tim, while he searched the rest of the flat. Tim disobeyed his orders and joined him in the search, except the search was soon over and both men stood still by the bedroom door. Libbie was lifeless on the bed. A stream of blood came out of her temple — the same gun she had used to kill her husband and her lover still hot in her hand.

51

24 DECEMBER 2016 - TWO MONTHS LATER

The latest events had left a deep mark in the life of the entire Seacross community and an even deeper mark in the life of Bernadette and the ones close to her. Facing Shane and Samuel with the entire truth was the most frightening thing she had ever done but for the first time in decades, she felt free. What Bernadette confessed was the answer to all the questions Shane had always wanted to ask her. It had not been the answer he was expecting, but after the initial feeling of loss and betrayal, it was the best one he could have had. In the beginning, he had been angry with Bernadette for everything she took away from him over the last twenty-three years. He didn't want to see her or talk to her, then he understood why she did what she did and even if he wanted to, he could not stop loving her. There was still time to build their life and family together. Samuel didn't hate his mother, even if she had raised him in a big lie. Bernadette was sure he would never forgive her, but she was wrong.

"I know I should be furious with you, Mom, and I should feel confused and betrayed like my whole world has been turned upside down, but I don't. I am feeling all right for the first time in a long time. Don't get me wrong. I loved Dad, but for some reason, I always felt a distance between us. A distance I always thought was there because of something I might have done."

"Oh, darling, nothing is wrong with you. It is all my fault."

"I mean it, Mom, I never felt I belonged to Dad as I did to you, and now I know why."

That conversation with Samuel still made Bernadette's eyes fill with tears and tears were filling her eyes tonight too, but for the first time in a long while, they were tears of joy.

Standing by the kitchen door with a glass in her hand, Bernadette stared at the room filled with the people she loved the most. These people were now her family.

"I never realised how much he looks like his father," Jane said, slipping her arm under her friend's. Bernadette looked straight across the room to where Shane and Sam were opening another bottle of Prosecco and smiled.

"Yes, he does."

ABOUT THE AUTHOR

Sabina Gabrielli Carrara is an Ireland-based Italian writer of psychological thrillers and murder mysteries. Her books are also available in Danish and soon will be in Italian.

After a degree in history and philosophy and some experience in human resources, the author moved to Ireland in 2003 where she is living in the little village of Balrothery with her husband, their two daughters and three dogs.

Fields Of Lies is Sabina's debut novel.

ALSO BY SABINA GABRIELLI CARRARA

Black Souls

The Last Witch, A Seacross Mystery (Book 1)

For more information on Sabina and her books, see her website at https://www.sabinagabriellicarraraauthor.com/

Printed in Great Britain
by Amazon

54780257R00129